TURNING YOURSELF AROUND

▼   ▼   ▼

READY TO TURN THINGS AROUND?
SYLVIA, JASON, AND KATHY WERE.

Jason, age 18: He started drinking when his parents divorced but powerfully denied his problem. Even intervention and a stay at a clinic were not enough to change Jason—it had to come from within.

Sylvia, age 16: "My whole life feels like a giant cover-up," she said at her first OA meeting. "I actually plan my social life around where and when I can binge .... I can't stand the deception anymore."

Kathy, age 17: She was scared and cut off from her family. After years of acting out, she finally turned to a friend, and for the first time began to see that she had been the victim of sexual abuse ....

THEY TURNED IT AROUND. SO CAN YOU.

Using the issue-by-issue exercises and self-tests in this book, along with a Twelve-Step program, teenagers can see their behavior for what it really is, confront its causes, and begin to live a clean and sober life one day at a time.

More About the Author

Kendall Johnson regularly lectures and gives seminars on crisis management, the effects of trauma and disaster upon children, and teacher trauma and self-care for school personnel, mental health professionals, and emergency caregivers. He also gives advanced training for school crisis response teams, and interventions for emergency incident command teams. He has provided training and consultations nationwide.

Dr. Johnson is an adjunct faculty member of the California Specialized Training Institute (Governor's Office of Emergency Services), a Professional Advisory Board member of the Los Angeles Psychological Trauma Center, a critical incident stress advisor to the National Fire Protection Association, and a speaker for the American Critical Incident Stress Foundation.

Dr. Johnson's publications include papers on divorce mediation and child custody, crisis management in the schools, and family sculpture, a group intervention strategy. He is the author of *Classroom Crisis: A Readi-Reference Guide* and *Trauma in the Lives of Children: Crisis and Stress Management Techniques for Teachers, Counselors, and Student Service Professionals.* Two other books, *Reclaiming Your Future: Moving Beyond Trauma, Dependency, and Recovery* and *School Crisis Management: A Team Training Guide* will be available later this year. Along with Wendy Deaton, he is coauthor of a series of Growth and Recovery workbooks for children working through trauma incidents or growing up in traumatic situations.

Dr. Johnson lives with his wife and children in Claremont.

TURNING YOURSELF AROUND

Self-Help Strategies for Troubled Teens

▼ ▼ ▼

Kendall Johnson, Ph.D.

Library of Congress Cataloging-in-Publication Data:
Johnson, Kendall, 1945-
Turning yourself around : self-help strategies for troubled teens / by Kendall Johnson
p.   cm.
ISBN 0-89793-092-4 : $9.95
1. Self-help techniques for teenagers. 2. Teenagers—Mental health.
3. Twelve-step programs—Miscellanea. I. Title.
RJ505.T84J64   1992
155.5—dc20   92-4477   CIP

Editorial coordinator: Lisa E. Lee
Copyeditor: Gina Renée Gross
Cover design: Qalagraphia
Cover artwork: Tamra Goris Designs
Production manager: Paul J. Frindt
Publisher: Kiran S. Rana
Set in Cheltenham and Helvetica by 847 Communications, Alameda, CA

9   8   7   6   5   4   3   2   *First edition*

Table of Contents

ACKNOWLEDGEMENTS

Special thanks are due to Scott Sullender and Verne Jahnke for their chapter reviews and comments, and to the students of San Antonio High School for their openness, persistence, and courage.

I'm not sure which is harder, writing books or publishing them. I do know that this book is truly a joint endeavor, and would not have even approximated its present incarnation without the wily eye of publisher Kiran Rana, the production artistry of Paul Frindt, editorial judgment of Gina Gross, and especially the enthusiasm, diplomacy, and continued inspiration of Lisa Lee. To all these people—and others at Hunter House—I owe a debt of gratitude.

DISCLAIMER

The material in this book is intended to provide a guide for dealing with problem behavior and addiction. Any exercises described should be undertaken with the guidance or under the supervision of a licensed therapist or Twelve-Step practitioner. The publisher, author, and editors cannot be held responsible for any errors or omissions. The author and publisher assume no responsibility for any outcome of the use of these materials in self-care programs or in use by a professional.

If you have any questions or concerns about the use or appropriateness of any materials in this book, we strongly recommend that you consult a licensed therapist.

Introduction

What brings you to this book? Did you find it on a shelf, and find yourself drawn to the title? Did someone recommend it to you? Either way, it will hold something for you. This book is about change.

Maybe everything is fine in your life. If so, fine! You don't need this book. Save your time! This book is for people who have things going on in their lives that they don't like, things they want to turn around.

What sorts of things? How about a full year of school with no credit earned? Or a D- average? Or a family life that is falling apart? Or social drinking or using which is becoming a more serious problem? How about uncontrolled eating binges, or not eating enough of the right things? Or not eating enough at all? How about having a group of friends who pressure you to do things that aren't in your best interest? How about not being able to finish anything you set out to do? How about thinking about taking your own life? These sorts of things.

Maybe some of these things are happening in your life, but you really aren't ready to do anything about them. That's your choice. Don't start this book. You won't put the necessary time in, and it won't change anything. And save your money, you'll need it. But if you're tired of the way things are, and you're ready to do some serious thinking about change, read on . . . .

What exactly does it mean to "turn yourself around"? It means to stop any destructive behavior. It means to stop doing some of the things that are creating friction in your life. It means breaking your dependencies. But it also means more. It means taking the first steps toward personal growth, productivity, and satisfaction. It means becoming the person you are meant to be!

This book is meant to be used as a supplement to a Twelve-Step recovery program. It follows the Twelve Steps of Alcoholics

Anonymous, the single most powerful recovery program in the world. The Twelve Steps have been tried by and have worked for literally millions of people who suffer from alcoholism, drug addiction, eating disorders, compulsive gambling, smoking, dependency upon self-destructive relationships, over-spending, sexual addiction, workaholism, and other compulsive problems. If it can work for these people, chances are it can work for you.

A NOTE ON THE TWELVE STEPS

The Twelve Steps were designed by two alcoholics who worked together to overcome their addiction and regain balance in their lives. They recorded the steps they had followed over the course of their recovery and their original Twelve Steps read as follows:

1. We admitted we were powerless over alcohol—that our lives had become unmanageable.

2. Came to believe that a Power greater than ourselves could restore us to sanity.

3. Made a decision to turn our will and our lives over to the care of God *as we understood Him.*

4. Made a searching and fearless moral inventory of ourselves.

5. Admitted to God, to ourselves, and to another human being the exact nature of our wrongs.

6. Were entirely ready to have God remove all these defects of character.

7. Humbly asked Him to remove our shortcomings.

8. Made a list of all persons we had harmed, and became willing to make amends to them all.

9. Made direct amends to such people wherever possible, except when to do so would injure them or others.

10. Continued to take personal inventory and when we were wrong promptly admitted it.

11. Sought through prayer and meditation to improve our conscious contact with God *as we understood Him,* praying only for knowledge of His will for us and the power to carry that out.

12. Having had a spiritual awakening as the result of these steps, we tried to carry this message to alcoholics, and to practice these principles in all our affairs.

(Permission to reprint the Twelve Steps of Alcoholics Anonymous granted by Alcoholics Anonymous World Services)

Over the years since Alcoholics Anonymous was formed, these steps brought sobriety, recovery, and serenity to millions of people worldwide. Gradually, these steps also came to be used by other groups in dealing with other addictive and compulsive behavior. This is because they represent an approach to dealing with problems that is inherently therapeutic.

Many young people, however, deny themselves the assistance of these twelve steps to freedom. Written in the 1930s, the steps reflect a culture that nowdays seems out-dated. The spiritual language of the steps seems to require a certain theology, including a God who is male. The steps appear to be written for alcoholics only. Finally, because the steps were written originally as a report, they read awkwardly. Thus many people are so put off by the original language that they cannot relate to the very process that could save them.

For these reasons, this book uses an adapted version of A.A.'s Twelve Steps. The revised steps directly follow the spirit of the original program, but use language which is:

▼ problem-neutral, and easily applied to problems other than alcohol

▼ theology-neutral, and fits a wide variety of spiritual orientations

▼ gender-equal, and does not claim that God is male

▼ personalized, focusing on the reader

The revised steps used in this book read as follows:

3

1. Admit your powerlessness over your problem and your inability to manage your life.

2. Come to believe that a power greater than you can restore you to strength.

3. Make a decision to turn your will and life over to the care of your Higher Power.

4. Make a searching and honest moral inventory of yourself.

5. Admit to your Higher Power, yourself, and to another human being the exact nature of your mistakes.

6. Prepare to have your Higher Power remove all of your limitations.

7. Humbly ask your Higher Power to remove all of your limitations.

8. Make a list of all the persons you have harmed, and become willing to make amends to all of them.

9. Make direct amends to these people wherever possible, except when it would hurt them or others.

10. Continue to make a personal inventory and when you are wrong admit it promptly.

11. Use prayer and meditation to improve your conscious contact with your Higher Power, trying to understand that Power's will and asking for the power to carry that out.

12. Try to use the insights you have gained through your spiritual awakening to carry this message to others who are in trouble.

In the pages that follow you will discover how and why these steps really work. You will experience the power of admitting weakness, the strength gained through honest self-appraisal, the relief brought about by apology and restitution, the joy of health, and the freedom of independence. These steps follow the natural logic of healing and employ the main strategies of self-change used by therapists the world over. The steps harness a higher power—your *own* higher power—and channel it into your life.

You can use this book as part of a Twelve-Step group program, whether residential or not. Or it can be used for additional reading and exercises apart from your participation in a group. It can also be used as a part of individual therapy. You can even use it alone, although Twelve-Step group participation is usually much more effective. If you do use it alone, be sure to complete all exercises that require you to do things with others.

When people talk about the various problems they are trying to overcome, they often use certain related terms or use words interchangeably. This can be confusing. These terms are habit, problem, compulsion, addiction, and compulsive behavior, and it may be helpful at this point to explain how they are used in this book.

Think about specifically what problem brought you to read this book. It may be an eating problem, a drinking problem, a problem with relationships, or a problem with drug use. In this book, the term "problem" will be used to refer to whatever if is you are struggling with. So if you have a drinking problem, whenever the book refers to "your problem," you should take it to refer to your drinking. "Problem behavior," thus, will refer to your drinking behavior.

The other words have slightly different meanings. "Habit" is when a person turns frequently to a specific problem behavior. "Compulsion" means that the person has difficulty resisting the problem behavior, and "compulsive behavior" refers to the behavior itself rather than their state of mind. "Addiction" means that doing without the problem behavior causes the person great discomfort and distress. This is true whether the problem is a substance such as alcohol, an action such as eating, or a situation such as a relationship. Addiction is often used to imply physiological or tissue dependency, as in substance addiction, however in this book it will not be limited in this way. "Dependency" refers to a condition of needing the object of the dependency in order to experience a sense of well-being. Thus "dependency" can be used interchangeably with "compulsion" or "addiction."

Two other words that will show up later in the text are "dysfunctional" and "enabling." "Dysfunctional" means that something is not working the say it should. Dysfunctional individuals are unable to perform the way they want to. When a family or group is dysfunctional, its members interact in a way that is self-defeating. "Enabling" is any response which allows dysfunction to continue. An enabler is someone who unintentionally makes it easier for another person to stay addicted, compulsive, self-defeating, or whatever they do that is dysfunctional.

The chapters of this book follow the Twelve Steps in sequence. They also follow the personal stories of three young people, Sylvia, Jason, and Kathy, and their progress through the Twelve Steps. Each chapter updates the progress of the three, provides insights into the importance of the particular step, and encourages you to do the exercises which will help you work through that step. Additional chapters deal with important issues such as prior trauma, loss, families, and relapse.

You may feel tempted to skip over some of the exercises, meaning to come back to them later. Try to resist doing this. The exercises are the real heart of the book and can help you sort out a lot of issues from your past. You can answer most of the questions in the space provided. If you need more room to write, keep a special notebook in which you write the longer answers and any related thoughts or ideas that might come up. You can also use this notebook as a journal, to record the good times and bad times as you work through this program.

However you use this book, use it honestly. There is no way this book, or any program, can help you if you are not honest. This may be a problem for you, or for anyone whose life needs to be turned around. Part of the difficulty of dealing with problems is that we are all human. This means that we do the best we can to survive. In order to overcome our difficulties, we learn to minimize them, to ignore our own complaints. We deny the size of the problem.

Overcoming this denial is hard. We have to learn to stop lying to ourselves and to others. We have to learn to trust our own strength and ability to handle adversity. To the extent you can be honest with yourself when working each chapter, you will profit from its perspectives and gain additional strength.

Good luck with this book! I hope that it can help you find what you seek—recovery from whatever is costing you your life. I wish you every success in turning your life around.

1

Three Lives in Trouble

Getting in serious trouble usually takes a while. We get there in steps, a little at a time. What begins as an experiment becomes several experiments. Several experiments become a pattern. We learn that we can gain temporary relief from stress. The pattern becomes a way of coping. What is useful as a way of coping becomes a habit. The habit becomes an identity—a part of ourselves. Before we realize it we have an addiction. We need the habit to live, and it keeps us from living.

We have found that certain habits have helped us get through. With some of us the problem can be alcohol or drugs. With some it can be an eating disorder, or taking big risks. Some of us become dependent upon love relationships. Whatever the problem, it is often the way we try to handle the pressures in our lives.

These are temporary solutions, stopgaps. They help us get through one crisis and then another. They are tempting because —in the short run—they work. We wouldn't use them if they didn't.

By the time we figure out that we are in trouble, the habit can be extremely difficult to break. What started as a way of dealing with our problems has become the problem itself. The solutions have become problems, and the problems seem to have no solutions. At this point, things can seem bleak. We feel that we are boxed in. But this is not true. What seems like a dead end may really be a crossroads.

SYLVIA G., AGE 16

The school library was just about deserted at 2:00 P.M. Sylvia had just eaten three candy bars and a small box of cookies, while she sat at a table behind the rows of literature books near the back corner of the room. Her initial feeling of relief and well-being, however, was quickly giving way to guilt and panic. She knew she would have to do something soon, or it would all go to fat. "Why did I have to eat those so soon?" she berated herself. It was still an hour until school let out, and she had an appointment at 3:30. Would the bathroom be safe?

Over the past several weeks, while approaching semester finals, Sylvia became more and more dependent upon food. She would carry junk food in her book bag, and munch away quietly. She hit upon the library during sixth period by accident, but Sylvia soon learned that it was the perfect place to hide. She found herself returning more and more. She felt sick from the food in her stomach. She couldn't wait. Sylvia started toward the restroom.

▼　▼　▼

Sylvia has an eating disorder. She is bulimic. Although she is concerned about her weight, she goes on eating binges. This compulsive behavior causes her to eat large amounts of food, which she then vomits. Sometimes, if she feels she is getting fat, she uses laxatives. She undereats, overeats, binges, and purges. She is always trying various diets and exercise programs in a desperate attempt to feel good about herself.

So far she has been careful to hide the binging from her family and friends. She buys and hoards food of her own with baby-sitting money, although she sometimes has to steal money to eat. Sylvia plans times for binging when no one will be around. Baby-sitting evenings are a good time, as are Tuesday nights when her parents are always out. Sometimes Sylvia will even cut afternoon classes to go home when she knows her mother will be away.

Sylvia's parents are perfectionists, and very controlling. They set her up to be anxious and self-doubting. Her father is a dentist, and her mother does not work. She is active, however, in political and charity work in the community. Both are concerned about their social status, and make it clear to Sylvia that she must marry well. Sylvia turns to food gratification to relieve anxiety.

Sylvia feels the pressure to succeed. She manages to keep her grades up, but constantly feels that she must be on the lookout for potential criticism. While some people go through life looking for opportunities, Sylvia looks for threats. Life to her is a minefield. Wherever she steps, she is afraid of being caught doing something wrong or being labeled inadequate. Sometimes Sylvia feels that no matter how hard she tries, her life could never be enough.

Her friends are in the more popular, socially correct crowd. Social status seems more important to her mother than anything else, and Sylvia has allowed her mother to pick her friends. She doesn't feel comfortable with her mother's choices, however, and does not get close to people. As a result, she has no one to confide in, and no one with whom she can share the truth about her problem.

JASON S., AGE 18

Jason turned off the ignition and just sat in the parking lot. Classes had already begun, but he was contemplating cutting again. He felt sick, but the beer he was sipping would help that. He had just about decided to split when he remembered that Aaron had his portable tape player and tape. He decided to go to second period, pick up his stuff, and then leave. The six-pack would take the morning to finish off.

Sipping his beer discreetly, Jason waited for the bell to ring. He would go in between first and second period and find Aaron. He figured he might not even have to stay for class. Just before the bell rang, Jason got out of the car and started toward the steps . . . .

▼   ▼   ▼

Jason started drinking in junior high school. It was sort of a rebellion thing at first. His parents were divorcing, and Jason had to fend for himself a lot. He figured he didn't have much to lose. He cut school with friends and got into whatever trouble he wanted. Trouble included alcohol, and Jason did his best to keep up with the rest. While he messed around with various other drugs, he always seemed to come back to drinking. Later he found that alcohol helped him endure the loneliness when his friends were no longer there.

9

Jason's parents have always fought. Nobody really knows if they are still married. They reconcile periodically, and tell Jason that everything is fine. Later, they fall apart, and he is expected to choose sides again.

Jason stands as a symbol of the difficulties his parents have. In their battling back and forth, he is the victim. Instead of working with him and recognizing the trouble he is having, they are content to let him retreat to his room. He has painted his room black, put up posters, and spends most of his time there.

In junior high school, Jason developed a new group of friends who encouraged him to cut classes and drink. They partied and got in trouble together. Aaron, Sammy, and Jason were called the Three Musketeers. They were almost like a family.

Now in high school, he attends enough classes to keep from getting in trouble, and pulls D grades. Alcohol helps him tolerate school, as well as control his own anger. Lately though, it's getting more and more difficult to stay in school. His teachers are pressuring him, the Three Musketeers are getting in bigger trouble, and the other kids are avoiding them. It is a whole lot easier to get wasted.

KATHY W., AGE 17

"Actually," began the Anglo princess with purple hair and striped leggings, "I've been thinking of going out with women instead of guys." Kathy had a penchant for the dramatic.

Silence. Shifting.

"You what?" asked the black girl in feigned indignation, mostly for her friend's benefit. She couldn't have cared less, but it was a great opportunity for a forum.

"You heard me. You really should try it."

"For real?" chimed in a third. The class dissolved in derisive laughter. Kathy had managed to shoot herself in the foot again. This was not the first time.

By the time the teacher had gotten things quieted down after Kathy's incident, two students had been sent to the principle's office. When the snickers and hard looks were over, the depression set in again. Now she would have to wait for the inevitable call to see the principal. Of course, her mother would then go ballistic. She always did.

Unable to bear another call to the principal's office over a class incident, Kathy decided to leave early. She would miss only the last two periods, and she could take enough time getting home that maybe her mother wouldn't notice. Maybe everyone would even forget.

After the bell rang, Kathy left school. She started home but decided to stop by the drug store where there was a phone. Her boyfriend Kyle was at work, but she had to talk to someone. Kyle didn't like getting calls at the auto shop because he was still a probationary employee. He had told her before not to call. His boss picked up the phone. "Yeah, just a minute," he said. She could hear him call out across the shop, "Kyle! It's your girlfriend again!" She knew it was a mistake to have called.

"Look," Kyle said directly without even a "hello," "I told you not to call me here!"

"I know," Kathy whined, "but I just had to talk to you. How's it going?"

"I'm busy, that's how. What do you want?"

"I just left school. I got into an argument, you know . . . "

"I don't have time, Kathy, I'll call you later."

"What time?" Kathy's voice reflected her uncertainty.

"I don't know! Goodbye already." Kyle was getting angry.

Not picking up his agitation, Kathy pressed forward. "Just tell me what time you'll call," she demanded.

"Forget it!" he yelled into the phone and slammed down the receiver.

Forget it? What does that mean? Forget it—don't worry about it? Forget it—I don't want to talk? Forget it—it's over? Kathy's rising panic overwhelmed her and she fought the impulse to call Kyle back. She hurried out of the drug store, suddenly aware that people were staring at her.

▼   ▼   ▼

From the way she looks you would think that she is a prostitute if you met her on the street. She isn't. Kathy is a codependent. She is desperate to be loved, and continually suffers abuse from the shallow and unrewarding relationships into which she throws herself.

She constantly competes for attention when she is in groups. She dresses outrageously, does her hair outrageously, says and does outrageous things, all in an attempt to remain the center of things. To her dismay she is ridiculed and disliked as a result of her constant bids for attention.

Her love relationships suffer as well. Kathy goes out with anyone who shows any interest in her. Because of her posture of desperation, she attracts boys who are only interested in what she can do for them. She accepts whatever they wish to do to her. Because she acts like a victim and is unable to protect herself, Kathy is victimized.

Kathy is confused by her social relationships. She doesn't understand why her every move backfires. During those moments when she realizes what is happening, she does have some sense that her actions are self-destructive, but she is unable to translate that insight into protective action. The anxiety she feels about possible abandonment quickly overrides any indignity she might experience at the hands of others.

Her parents have been divorced for years, and both are remarried. Kathy is shuttled back and forth between the two houses, a distance of some five hundred miles. She spends the majority of her time with her mother and stepfather, who moved in shortly after they were married. There was much fighting in the original marriage, and when Kathy's parents divorced they fought over her. This lasted as long as the court fight, and then they worked at controlling each other through her. Finally, as her father, and later her mother, found someone else and began new families, Kathy became a burden to them. Perhaps it was because they didn't want a constant reminder of the painful past, or perhaps their present relationships could not withstand the stress of a stepchild. Whatever the reason, Kathy is not really wanted in either house. She is tolerated and ignored until she becomes a problem, and then she is shipped back to the other parent's house.

Having married early, Kathy's parents were both immature. Her mother's pregnancy was unplanned and unwelcome. They were unhappy to begin with and their relationship compounded their unhappiness. When Kathy was born, neither parent was able to bond well with her. When the divorce occurred, she was not wanted by either. She has been fighting those feelings of abandonment ever since.

2

Admissions: Step One

Sylvia, Jason, and Kathy are in trouble. Sylvia has allowed her eating behavior to become compulsive and has withdrawn from friends and family to hide her eating. Jason has let his drinking become more and more important to him. His school attendance and performance are suffering, and even his friends are beginning to write him off. Kathy is so lost in her cloud of social anxiety and attempts to control others that she is an object of ridicule and scorn. Sylvia is about to lose her real friends, Jason is about to be kicked out of school, and Kathy is about to get a surprise at home. Their lives are out of control.

Before they can begin to turn their lives around, before they can start to take advantage of the help that is available to them, they must first admit the bottom line fact that they have problems, and that their problems are beyond their control. Step One reads:

1. Admit your powerlessness over your problem and your inability to manage your life.

Admission sometimes occurs through insight. Sometimes it occurs through confrontation with others. Sometimes it takes an actual hospital admission before you will acknowledge what is clear to others. It's not easy to admit that you have a problem. Or that the problem is bigger than you. We all like to feel that we are in control of our lives, that we can manage our own affairs. But if we are no longer in control, if our problem is more powerful than we are, and if we really cannot manage our lives, the road to recovery must begin with admission.

SYLVIA

"Oh my gosh," thought Sylvia, "I thought they were gone!" She sat in the library bathroom breathlessly listening.

Someone was still there, also listening.

"Yuck!" came a voice. "That is so gross!"

"Wait," answered another, "maybe she needs help. Are you all right?" she directed to Sylvia.

Sylvia remained silent. She had heard the crowd come in, and waited until she heard the restroom door close behind their exit before making herself throw up again. She had assumed they were all gone, but apparently she was wrong. "Boy," she thought to herself, "How wrong could I get? They're going to tell the whole school. That was really dumb."

"Are you alright?" the second voice persisted. "Shall we call the nurse?"

"No, I'm OK. Well, I just feel a little sick, but don't call the nurse." They were not going to leave, and she couldn't sit there any longer without them calling the nurse. Pulling herself together, Sylvia rose to face them. She prayed that it wouldn't be too obvious. She walked out of the stall and brushed past Sally Jenkins and Louise Parker. "I'm fine," she murmured. Sally and Louise! Sally would have it all over the campus in no time at all. Sylvia walked out of the library, past the office, and off campus. No way was she going to stay!

Tears flowed as she walked slowly toward home. She was humiliated. She could just hear it tomorrow: "Did you hear about Sylvia? She's a 'Scarf and Barf!'" There would be no hiding the truth. Maybe she could get some cookies and ice cream before she got home. No, her mother was there! The feeling of panic rose again, constricting her throat and making her take deep breaths. "What am I doing?"

She had stopped walking. There was no place to go. She sat down on a low wall and cried. Everything seemed to speed up. It felt as if the world was spinning around her.

"Sylvia!" Louise stood before her, breathing heavily after running to catch up with Sylvia. "What's wrong?"

Sylvia looked at her through red eyes. "Nothing, why?"

"Sylvia, I think you may have a problem." Louise looked at Sylvia compassionately. "You know, last year I went through some hard times myself. I've seen you eating. I used to do that myself."

Sylvia didn't know what to say.

"I got help, Sylvia. I think you need help now."

Sylvia looked down. She couldn't deny it any longer. "I don't know what to do about it."

JASON

"Jason, could I see you for a minute?" Coach Harwick had stepped in Jason's way as he cruised down the hallway looking for Aaron. Students moved around them on their way to classes.

"What's up, Coach?" began Jason. "I've got to get to class."

"Come in here a minute." The coach escorted Jason into a conference room near the counselors' offices. "Someone wants to see you." Jason rolled his eyes, feigning boredom. Actually, he was off balance. Coach was usually forceful, but this time it was different. There was no questioning him. And why the conference room? Jason's radar went up.

He walked in the room and was taken aback. His parents were there. So was his counselor, Ms. Privitt. He looked around. His sister Jeanne was sitting next to Mr. Samuelson, whom he worked for in the garage after school. Two friends he had known for a long time, Timmy and Elizabeth, were sitting by someone he did not know. Something was definitely wrong.

Jason turned to leave. Coach blocked his way. "Sit down, Jason. We'd like to talk to you." Jason sank into the only remaining seat.

"Jason, my name is Mike . . . . " began the stranger. "I'm a counselor at Haven House. It's a rehab hospital."

Jason stared blankly at Mike. He was beginning to get the picture now. "What is this?"

Mike glanced around at the other members of the small group. He was dressed in comfortable clothes and looked alert but relaxed. "Jason, these people have asked me to conduct a very special meeting with you this morning. They each have something important to say to you that they want you to hear."

Jason did not speak. Even breathing was a little difficult. He was beginning to feel trapped. He had a strong urge to get up and get out of the room. Coach was sitting in front of the door.

"These people are the important people in your life, Jason," Mike continued, "Each is going to take a turn. Coach Harwick is going to be first."

Jason had never played football, but he had taken PE with Coach. Harwick was demanding, and sometimes had ridden Jason's case about not dressing in gym clothes, but he had always been fair, and had listened to him the few times Jason had wanted to talk.

"Jason," started Coach, "I've known you for a year and a half. I've liked you, at least until lately. Since the start of this year, you've been a problem to me. You're either a no-show or you don't dress out, or else you blow off everything I say. You start trouble with other kids. Some days you're OK, but the next day you're in some other world with a chip on your shoulder. You make fun of me, you pull down the whole class, and you're just too much trouble." Coach paused.

Jason blinked. Coach had never talked to him like this before. "Look, Coach," he tried.

"Jason," Coach interrupted, "on the days that you're a problem, I can smell alcohol on you. I've mentioned it before, but it hasn't made a bit of difference."

"I only . . . " Jason tried again.

"I see you going downhill fast," said Harwick. "You're losing my respect and the respect of your friends. I think you've got a big problem. You're a drunk. You think you cover it up, but you don't. It all boils down to this, Jason: you take care of business and get straight. I don't want you back in my class unless you do."

Jason was stunned. He was hurt and angry. Who the hell did Coach think he was? Jason looked around at the others. They sat looking directly at him. "What's going on?" he demanded.

"Jason," Mike replied, "Ms. Privitt, your school counselor, has something to say."

Each of the adults took a turn. Ms. Privitt told Jason about his grades, the incident reports he had received from teachers, and his options. His friends told him about how he had withdrawn from them, and how they were about to give up on him unless something big changed.

His mother was last. She recounted one incident after another when Jason's actions had caused her pain and how it was getting worse, not better. "Things have grown intolerable," she concluded, "we cannot continue this way. We want you to enter the Haven House program this morning. That's the only way you can earn your way back into our house."

Jason could not believe it. They were just trying to get rid of him. The anger started to flare up again, but Jason felt his defenses weaken. He sat there, becoming increasingly numb and detached. There was no use trying to leave. There was no use fighting it. One thing is sure, Jason thought, things are definitely out of control.

KATHY

That afternoon Kathy gritted her teeth as she walked in the front door of her home. She knew better than to expect a "welcome home," but she was hoping to avoid a fight.

"Kathy." Her mother's voice called from the kitchen. Kathy started up the stairs to her room.

"Kathy!" She hesitated. There was a different tone in her mother's voice. Puzzled, Kathy proceeded to her room, still hoping it would blow over.

Her suitcase was sitting outside the door to her room. Her heart sank. The same ugly green suitcase that she had to use whenever she was sent back to her father's home. Images of airport lines, impersonal attendants, and waves of familiar emptiness flooded her. Kathy stumbled into the bathroom and locked the door. It was happening again. Her bedroom door would be locked. The tickets would be on the dinner table. Not much would be said. She would be driven to the airport and sent off to her father's in Fresno.

Fresno, California. Her father would look distressed, his wife would cover her obvious resentment with a plastic smile, and her stepsisters would be planning revenge. The kids at Union High School—where nothing exciting ever happened—would hate her. She had seen it all before, over and over.

Maybe not, she thought. Kathy had $100 in her purse, which she had saved from baby-sitting. She unlocked the door quietly, walked back into the hall, and picked up her suitcase. She carried it down the stairs. "Kathy, come here!" yelled her Mom, as Kathy softly closed the front door behind her.

Kathy caught a bus downtown. People stared at her and her suitcase, but that was nothing new. The $100 wasn't much, she

17

thought. It should last a few days, though. Maybe something would happen. She found an inexpensive hotel, and checked in. It was dingy, granted, but it would only be for a couple of nights. Something had to happen by then.

Three days later a great deal had happened, but she was still in the crummy little hotel room. Worse, the $100 was just about gone. Kathy walked the streets looking for work, fearful that she might be spotted by her parents, the police, or worse, her friends. She was starting to get depressed.

Two pimps had attempted to befriend her, but she wasn't that desperate. At least she wasn't yesterday. Today she was down to the last of her money. Her applications had not gotten her jobs, and she was down to two choices: sell herself or go home. She decided to go home.

Kathy spent the last of her money on the bus ride home. She was a failure. She had blown school, had blown the whole social scene, had never held a regular job, and couldn't make it on her own. It was time to admit defeat and throw herself at the mercy of her mother. After all, it couldn't be all that bad, could it? Some heartfelt apologies, promises to do better, assurances that her mother had been right. She could handle it.

The door was locked. She tried her key. It wouldn't work. Kathy sat down on the steps and waited, fighting back her tears and the cold feeling inside. It began to get dark.

Her mother's car pulled into the driveway. Kathy brightened. "Hi Mom!" she called.

Kathy's mother looked at her darkly. "Kathy, you are no longer welcome in this house. Please leave."

"But Mom, I . . . " pleaded Kathy. Her mother pushed by her into the house, locking the door behind her.

After waiting for an hour on the steps, Kathy started to walk with her heavy suitcase. She moved aimlessly down sidewalks. She walked for blocks. "What's happening to me," she thought. "Why do I keep messing things up?"

Then she thought of Nicole. A quiet girl, Nicole was in several of Kathy's classes. They had talked several times. Nicole had told her that she had been through some sort of difficulty. Kathy had been impressed by Nicole's inner calmness. It was as if she knew a wonderful secret. Nicole had told her that if she ever needed help to let her know.

Kathy had been confused by that remark at the time, but now she understood.

Kathy found Nicole's address in a telephone book in a booth. She found her way and walked up the steps. The doorbell chimes were comforting. Nicole opened the door. "Hi Kathy, what's wrong?"

"Nicole," Kathy began, "I need your help."

INSIGHTS

Being stuck is a drag. It's realizing that things have gotten worse than you thought. It's trying to quit doing something you thought you could quit, and then finding out you can't. It's discovering that you haven't been fooling anyone. It's finding out that you don't have the power you thought you had.

Nobody starts out wanting to get stuck. We don't get into trouble because we want to be bad. We get into drinking, smoking, taking pills, binge eating, running away, cutting school, breaking laws, and other sorts of trouble to make things better, not worse. For a while it's fun, real fun. Then it becomes routine. Then things get worse. It finally dawns on us that what started as a way to make things better isn't working any more. And worse, we have a habit.

So then we decide to quit. Maybe we can break the habit easily, and maybe not. We try to just stop, and we do for a while. Then we find ourselves back doing it again. We quit again. We start again. We may even start a program for a while. It works, so we quit the habit and the program. Then we start again. Pretty soon it dawns on us that quitting isn't so easy.

Part of the problem lies in your age. Adolescence is the time to declare to the world *who* you are in terms of your interests, friends, and lifestyle. But if you have been spending most of your time getting into trouble, becoming dependent, or becoming over-involved with a peer group, then it's hard to see your habit as a problem. If you do so, you deny much of your identity. To see your problem as a problem is to attack who you are. It seems easier to put up with your problem than to construct a whole new identity.

But that's a lot of BS. You know that you have a problem, or you wouldn't have read this far. If you wish to stay stuck, the best way is to continue to deny the problem. If you want to turn yourself around, however, the first step is often the hardest. You must admit and acknowledge what is wrong in your life.

Remember, you are not alone. Don't feel that you are the only person your age who has the sorts of problems you are experiencing. Look around! How many others do you know who are going through tough times? And just think about the number of people who have serious problems which you know nothing about. Growing up is hard and many young people get into difficulty. But take heart. A great many of these people have been able to turn those problems around. Lots of kids who look like they don't have problems are already overcoming them and are now in recovery.

EXERCISES

Let's size up your problem. Remember that it is very important at this step to be honest with yourself—brutally honest. Since the size of your problem will determine the size of the cure, it is easy to fall into the minimizing trap, which goes like this: you start by underestimating the size of the problem (after all, who wants to believe that his or her life is really unmanageable?). Then you make a plan of attack which is okay for smaller problems, but doomed to failure for your full-sized problem. Then you are surprised and defeated when your efforts don't do the job.

On the following pages are some questions to ask yourself. When you answer, fill the space with your response. Instead of short answers or vague generalizations, be as detailed and specific as you can. For example, instead of just saying

"relationship problems"

try to say something like

"I pick the wrong partner, take a lot of abuse, and end up more unhappy than before."

First, complete the following chart:

	Stressor	*Behavior*	*Result*
Sylvia	parent pressure	binge eating	social humiliation
Jason	school	alcohol addiction	isolation
Kathy	social anxiety	love addiction	self-defeat
You	_____	_____	_____

What is your problem behavior? What are you doing that needs to be turned around?

_____

_____

_____

_____

How long has it been going on?

_____

_____

_____

_____

How often does it occur?

_____

_____

_____

_____

Where and when does it happen?

_____

_____

_____

_____

Where 1 = a small problem and 10 = an overwhelming problem, rate your problem on a scale of 1 to 10:

_____

Before going on, think about how you did the previous exercise. If you were holding back, or listing a minor problem when you have a bigger one to deal with, let's reconsider. This is a chance to do something about it and to regain some strength and manageability in your life. Go back and try that last section again. Risk a little more! And if you don't want anyone else to see what you write, get out some paper or a notebook and do the exercises.

Sylvia hid her binging and her throwing up from everyone. Jason hid his drinking from some people. Do you engage in cover-ups? Have you hidden evidence? Lied?

_____

_____

_____

How have you felt doing that?

_____

_____

_____

How has your problem behavior violated your own personal standards?

_____

_____

_____

Have you experienced shame, embarrassment, or guilt for your actions?

_____

_____

_____

Do you find yourself doing things that you don't want to do?

_____

_____

_____

Have you lost things which were important to you (such as grades, possessions, jobs, or relationships) due to your problem? List them.

_____   _____

_____   _____

_____   _____

Have you gotten to the place where you are afraid you cannot stop your habit?

_____

_____

Are you afraid of doing what it would take to end your dependency?

_____

_____

You have probably decided that things are not working for you. And you have probably also decided to quit doing what you have been doing. Perhaps several times by now! Think about each time you tried to change your problem behavior in the past. Did you try the same ways each time? Did you use any special techniques? Were you involved in any programs?

_____

_____

_____

_____

_____

_____

23

How did it work?

_____

_____

_____

_____

What goes wrong with your attempts to change?

_____

_____

_____

What would it take for you to admit that you have "bottomed out," or that your life has become unmanageable?

_____

_____

_____

Has it happened yet?

_____

_____

_____

3

Turning It Over:
Steps Two and Three

It takes a great deal to admit our powerlessness over alcohol, drugs, food, relationships, or other compulsions. We can suffer for years, denying our suffering and blaming it upon others. Holding on to our delusions of control over our problems seems to be a source of strength and pride. Pride, yes. But this is the kind of false pride that has always been a problem for people.

Strength, no. Denial of weakness is not a source of strength. It robs us of energy and options. Denial keeps us from understanding just what we are up against. Military victories are never won by underestimating the enemies' strength or ignoring their tactics.

Step Two is clear:

2. Come to believe that a power greater than you can restore you to strength.

Our problem has made us act irrationally and against our own interests. By admitting our weakness in the face of the problem, we open ourselves to help from other sources. Our pride and mistaken belief that we can handle anything have resulted in our losing control. If we are unable to manage our lives, we need help to regain strength.

Where can this help come from? In the past, we relied upon negative friends, food, alcohol, risk, excitement, dependent relationships, stealing, or other immediate fixes to fill some need that we had. But our fixes aren't solutions any more, they have become problems. In order to deal with these powerful issues and meet our original needs, we need help. We must look toward a healthier and more positive power in our lives, and must come to believe that this power can actually help.

Step Three asks for that help:

> 3. Make a decision to turn your will and life over to the care of your Higher Power.

Step Three does not ask us to become saints. It does not ask us to have perfect belief. It does not even ask us to become religious. It simply asks us to make a decision. We must decide that we are not all-powerful ourselves. We must turn over our fate. We must be willing to work at putting our problems and our lives into the hands and care of a Higher Power.

Twelve-Step programs often surprise people. They expect to begin with admitting that they have a problem and then go right into fixing it. Yet Steps Two and Three back off and raise a different issue, one which seems to be off the track. Instead of looking further at the problem, the steps address spiritual concerns.

The way it works though, is that by admitting that our efforts have proven inadequate, and by invoking a power greater than ourselves, we put ourselves in the position to do what we could not do before, which is to make our problems manageable.

Sylvia

Sylvia was uncertain and didn't know what to say. Earlier, she had just been found out in the bathroom. Louise had just confronted her with her eating problem, and she felt as if her life had ended. By tomorrow most of the school would know. Yet strangely she felt a kind of peace inside. The fact that Louise knew brought her relief.

"Last year I was doing what you were doing, Sylvia. Everything was coming down on me, and I would eat. A lot! I was hiding it from everybody, and I was making myself throw up to keep from getting fat. That's what you were doing, wasn't it."

"Yes," replied Sylvia. Again, although she thought that the admission would make her feel worse, she felt better.

"It turned into a real compulsion," Louise continued. Pretty soon I was just living to eat. I didn't realize how bad I had gotten. I didn't eat to feel good, I was just eating to feel normal. People were avoiding me, and I was avoiding them. Let's walk . . . "

Sylvia picked up her books. "How did you quit?"

"A friend told me about Dr. Perez. She's a psychologist. I started going to her."

"How did she help?" Sylvia was clearly doubtful.

"She allowed me to talk about it, and a lot of other things. She told me about Overeaters Anonymous."

"What's that?"

"It's a group of people like us who have problems with eating. We meet on Thursdays."

Sylvia and Louise walked and talked for an hour. Sylvia realized that she could trust Louise, and that Louise had something that Sylvia wanted. Strength. Inner peace. A manageable life. She wanted to try whatever it was that had worked for Louise.

▼ ▼ ▼

"My name is Sylvia, and I'm just visiting." She paused. "I'm an overeater."

"Hi, Sylvia," answered the group.

"My gosh," she thought, "I said it."

The meeting had begun at 7:30 P.M. Some things had been read, and now people were introducing themselves. Most were overeaters, some were dependent upon other things. Each used just his or her first name and identified the particular problem.

As people shared their stories and their struggles, Sylvia was amazed. She heard herself described over and over. The names changed, the individual situations changed, but the pattern of dependency stayed the same. The feelings were the same. Pain and anxiety led to eating, eating led to shame, shame led to pain and anxiety. She heard stories of triumph. Members related their experiences in overcoming the bonds of compulsion.

It was too good to be true. She wanted to believe that this was a place she could safely be, a place where she could tell about what was happening to her without being laughed at or criticized. Yet, there was something going on with which she was having trouble.

"I had to let go of it," one woman was saying, "I just had to turn it over to God." "That's it," thought Sylvia. "I'm not a Christian. If I were a Christian, I could believe in God. But that would be a lie. I don't, and I'm not, and if that's what you have to be, then I can't."

After the meeting Sylvia was still troubled. "Louise, you have a faith that I just don't have. This is not going to work!" She felt the usual sense of panic returning.

"Why don't you try talking to Dr. Perez," suggested Louise. "She understands. Maybe she can help."

▼ ▼ ▼

The office was quiet. Dr. Perez sat in an easy chair across from Sylvia, her graying hair pulled back into a loose bun. Her eyes were gently probing, and she waited for Sylvia to think about the question she had just asked.

Sylvia felt disoriented. Something about the question had thrown her. She couldn't even remember what had been asked. "Could you repeat that?"

"I asked if you believed in chaos," repeated Dr. Perez.

"I don't understand."

"Well, some people think that things just happen in the world, without rhyme or reason. That's chaos. Others feel that there is some sort of purpose behind it all."

This was her third visit. Sylvia had immediately liked Dr. Perez and felt that she could share with her. Dr. Perez took her seriously. "I'm not sure," replied Sylvia.

And indeed she wasn't. She had fought against her parents over religion. They were strict Catholics, and had expected Sylvia to accept Catholicism without question. They had been thunderstruck when she had walked out of confirmation class. "Dr. Perez, I'm not a very religious person. I don't like church, with all its attitudes and judgments. My parents want me to go, but it seems so dishonest."

"So you don't believe in anything?"

"Well, I didn't say that." Sylvia thought some more. How could she say it?

"Sylvia," Dr. Perez pushed forward "maybe you aren't a religious person, but you certainly sound like a very spiritual one to me."

"How do you mean?"

"You seem to be looking for something. You seem to be demanding something of yourself and of the world. What do you expect?"

Ah! That's it. She couldn't imagine a world this complicated not having a reason or direction. She could not imagine a person in this world who did not have a place and role in it. "I guess I expect there to be a reason for my being here. I expect myself to find that reason, whatever it is, and make it happen."

"Then that's your god, Sylvia."

"Even though I don't know just what it is?"

"Even though . . . "

▼ ▼ ▼

"So," thought Sylvia on her way home from the session. "I don't have to 'be Christian' to be in that group." It was decided. She would return to the group on Thursday.

Sylvia realized that god could be a god of her choice, even a mystery god, and she could still believe that the group process helped. She had a mission in this world, and recovering from her eating problem was the first step in finding out what her purpose was.

Jason

Raindrops bounced off the wipers, then streamed down the windshield. Jason felt the car pull into the parking lot at Haven House. He looked beyond the window to the low-lying building which looked a little like a medical facility—lots of concrete, lots of glass you couldn't see through. Jason was numb, resigned to whatever would happen.

After admissions, the point system was explained. He was shown to his room, issued bedding, and given the speech about rules, motivation, and success. "Right," he thought, "I put in my time and get out of here."

▼ ▼ ▼

Eleven patients sat in a large circle. Mike was the leader. They were talking about sharing, but Jason sat quietly. One of the guys was being criticized by two of the girls.

"Look," said the guy, "I don't know what you're tweaked about, I listen to you every day, and I do care. I'm the one who's been on your side all along."

"That's not what this is about. Sure, you're always nice and listen, but that's not enough. We don't know who you really are. You never share who you are. Say something! Get mad!" The girl was intense.

"Jason, what do you think?" asked Mike. "Is it enough to be nice, or do we owe others more?"

Jason withdrew. "I pass," he finally managed.

"No way!" erupted the same girl who had been badgering the other guy.

"Wait a minute," Mike intervened. "Jason is new, let him get a chance to know you. It's time for lunch. Let's close for now, and we'll see you tomorrow."

At lunch, Jason sat across from his roommate, Duvall.

"Welcome to Hell House," Duvall tried.

Jason looked at him. "Yeah. Welcome home." Duvall was quiet. "How long have you been here?" asked Jason.

"Twenty-three days," answered Duvall.

"Drinking or drugs?"

"Both. I'm an addict. How about you?"

Jason paused. "They threw me in here because they didn't know what else to do with me."

"You know," replied Duvall, "it took me a long time to figure out that it wasn't someone else who had the problem."

At that, Jason got up and left. Walking down the hall he was still mad about Duvall's implication. "That's it," he thought, "I'm out of here. Tonight I go for it."

▼ ▼ ▼

Jason came to slowly. The horn that had brought him around was still blowing. Moonlight gave enough light for him to see, but it was hard to make sense of what he was looking at. Everything in the car was upside down and backwards. He stared at the ignition for several minutes, trying to figure out which way to turn it off. He didn't want to hit the starter, for fear of igniting any gas which might have spilled.

The effects of the whiskey didn't help, although the shock of the accident was now helping him focus. He kicked open the door and pulled himself out of the overturned car, almost falling because the hillside was so steep. Jason looked up the hill to the broken guardrail. "How in hell did I do that?"

Sirens. Jason pulled himself together. "If I get caught," he thought, "they'll either arrest me or send me back to rehab." He started up the hill. The headlights of a car swept the guardrail as someone drove up. Having second thoughts, Jason went back down the hill, past the car, and into the bushes beyond. He made his way down the canyon, hearing more cars arriving and people calling to each other as they started down the hill to the wrecked car.

Breaking out of rehab had been easier than he had expected. Getting money had been just as easy. He had broken into a house and taken what he wanted: fifty dollars and two bottles of whiskey. The open bottle had been nearly half full, but it didn't last long. By the time he had finished that, he had come across the sedan with the keys still in the ignition. He had been on his way to find the rest of the Musketeers when he had misjudged the turn and gone through the guardrail.

"Now what do I do?" he wondered. The shock was setting in, combining with the whiskey, and Jason felt shaky. He stumbled over a rock and landed in a bush. When he awoke this time it was even later. The moon had traveled across the sky. It was darker and colder.

"I've got to find some place to go," Jason thought as he started up again. Breaking and entering, grand theft auto, leaving the scene; he began to realize how serious things had gotten. They were probably looking for him. It was after 2:00 A.M. when he got to town. He was wondering what to do, when he looked up and found himself standing in front of the church he had attended as a child. The perfect place to hide! He let himself in the sanctuary restroom window which had been left open.

The sanctuary was quiet as Jason chose a pew toward the back. The pews were padded, and were just right for sleeping. He sat in the dim light, relaxing for a moment before laying down.

It was funny being in the church he had known so well. The religious symbols and icons were strangely comforting. He remembered sitting in the same seat years ago and thought how easy the world had seemed back then. He had loved the church and loved doing church things. If only his parents hadn't separated. He remembered them leaving the church; he had been nine years old. Although he had gotten used to living without church, he had really gotten mad when they got back together and joined another church. He refused to go. Now, sitting here in the quiet, Jason was reminded of what he had been missing.

So how was he going to get out of this mess? Absolutely nothing was working. He knew he was going to have to go back to the rehab center. But it was so fake. Those girls who were all over that guy. The motivation speech. It was clear that he needed help, but it wasn't clear where he was going to get it.

The church had always been a sanctuary in the past. He remembered the time just before his parents had first split up. There was much fighting in the house. He was frequently used as a pawn in the struggle raging between his parents. Several times he had snuck out and taken refuge in this very church. It had always seemed so peaceful and serene. A priest had actually noticed him and had spent hours talking about his troubles and about God's love for him.

Then it came to him. What he needed was right under his nose. The church. If he had the church to rely on, to sustain him again, he could get straight. It had worked for him before. It was about the only thing that had worked for him. And he knew that it would be the only thing that would work again. If he could get right with God, he could get through Haven House. And if he could do that, he could get back into the church, on his own, without his parents. With the church, he could get clean.

Relieved, and with a sense of satisfaction and direction, Jason lay down and went to sleep.

KATHY

"Kathy, come in" invited Nicole. "You look tired. Put your suitcase down. Can I get you anything to eat?" Kathy felt something release inside her. She didn't realize how tired she was. She let herself be drawn into the kitchen and given a late supper. She could hardly keep her eyes open, much less talk. Nicole made up a bed and steered Kathy into the shower.

"We'll talk in the morning." Nicole had said shortly before Kathy stumbled into bed. She drew the comforter up around her neck and fell into the deepest sleep she had had for days.

▼ ▼ ▼

When Kathy finally awoke she smelled breakfast cooking. She rolled over and looked around. The events of the previous day came back to her and she winced. It could hardly have been worse. She couldn't believe that yesterday she had been so desperate and now she was being taken care of so well.

Treating herself to another shower, Kathy started questioning herself. "How can I just relax and stop getting myself in such trouble?" she wondered. She thought of Nicole. What was it about Nicole that she admired so much? Nicole was relaxed, but it was more than that. There was some sort of inner calm. And pride, almost as if she knew something wonderful.

"Good morning, Kathy, I wasn't sure you were going to wake up!" Nicole had set the table and was putting a glass of juice down at Kathy's place. "Sit down and let's eat."

"Nicole . . . " began Kathy, searching for the right words to express her gratitude. "I don't know where I'd be if you hadn't taken me in last night."

"It's OK" replied Nicole. "Someone was there for me once. I'm glad I could help."

As they ate, they talked about many things. Finally Kathy was able to ask directly. "Nicole, there's something about you that I need to know. I don't know how to say this, but you seem to be so happy, and OK with yourself. I was thinking about that this morning, and how I am always trying to get people to like me."

"I've made a real mess of things," Kathy continued. "I don't know when to stop. I choose the wrong people and let myself get dumped on. No one seems to like me anymore. Even my own mother threw me out yesterday. I'm frantic trying to get people to like me, and I get nowhere. You don't seem to work at it, and you have plenty of friends. I just don't get it. You seem lit up from inside and happy. How do you do it?"

"Kathy, I'm not always happy. And I don't have all that many good friends. I used to try. I used to think that it was important to have all kinds of friends. I was a lot like you—*am* a lot like you. But I've learned that I have to like myself first or no amount of friends will be enough."

"How do you learn to like yourself?" asked Kathy. "In my case," she wondered to herself, "what's to like?"

"It took a while," said Nicole, "and the help of a couple of good friends. I had to learn that I was good enough the way I was. I had always thought that I had to win people's love. I never considered that they might have to win mine."

"But look at me," Kathy interrupted, "I can't do anything right. If I died now, no one would care. I've never done anything worthwhile."

"That's just what I mean," said Nicole. "I used to think that I had to do the things that other people wanted. I was afraid of losing their love and approval if I didn't."

"But people won't like you if you don't," tried Kathy.

"It depends upon who it is. Kathy, I like you whether or not you get over depending upon others. I would hope that you can get strong and stop holding others up to be your god, but I'm not going to like you any more or less because of it."

That stopped Kathy. "What do you mean 'holding others as my god'?"

"Well," answered Nicole, "if you see other people as more important than you are, and you take their wishes to be your commands, it sounds like you believe that they are gods."

"But I don't really believe in any god," protested Kathy.

"You act like it. Everybody has a god. With some people it's a biblical god, with some it's a job, and with some it's a bottle. With you it's other people."

Kathy thought about it. "What's your god?"

Nicole looked straight at Kathy. "This may be hard for you right now, but my god is my own Higher Self."

"What's that?" asked Kathy, who thought she might already know.

"For me, my Higher Self is the part of me that knows what is right or wrong, what's really best for me. It's who I am growing up to be."

All her life Kathy had looked for a Higher Power. She looked for God in others, because she couldn't believe in herself. But it was getting very obvious that it was not working for her. Kathy was getting ready for a new way of looking at things.

"My higher self," thought Kathy. "A god within. I wonder how I find it? Nicole mentioned that she was attending a support group for co-dependents. The CoDA group sounds interesting. If it works for her, who knows?" "Nicole," she asked, "can I go with you to your next meeting?"

INSIGHTS

Steps Two and Three require that we recognize a power higher than ourselves, and that we turn our problems over to that power for solution. While these steps are immediately comforting and helpful to some people, they put off others. Those who have trouble with these steps often give up on the entire Twelve-Step program. This is a tragic mistake.

It is a mistake because the Twelve Steps are the most successful recovery program there is. It is tragic because it is unnecessary. And it is unnecessary because you absolutely do not have to believe in the traditional church god to follow the Twelve Steps.

At first glance the language in the Twelve Steps suggests that you do. "God" is capitalized, referred to as a "He," and described as if "He" will take over and solve your problems if you just believe correctly. If that way of interpreting the language works for you, fine. Use it.

If not, look again. Consider substituting the term "higher power," "spirit," or "love" for "God". Jason's "Higher Power" was God. For Sylvia, on the other hand, the universe and her place in it was her "Higher Power." Kathy hasn't worked it all out yet, but her Higher Power is turning out to be her own Higher Self. This is a Higher Power which she is beginning to discover and will learn to trust.

If you have a dependency problem, you have already turned your problems over to a power greater than you, the habit or thing on which you are dependent. Steps two and three ask only that you form a relationship to a power *greater* than your dependency—a Higher Power.

Your God can be a Higher Power or lower power. Your God is whatever you give yourself over to. Up until now you may have let your problem be God. A "lower power" god could be an addiction such as food, alcohol, or love. Your "Higher Power" God can be anything to which you give yourself which can enhance your life, others, or the world.

You may have a traditional view of God. The way you conceive of God may have been taught to you in church, or through early family experience, and is reinforced by your reading of the Bible, the Koran, or other religious writings. Wonderful! As long as your relationship with God enhances you, others, and the world, what more could anyone ask?

You may have a non-traditional view of God, or perhaps you may not believe in a god at all. Yet you may have an interest or focus in your life that enhances you, others, and the world. You may be an athlete. You may study dance. You may devote yourself to serving others. As long as this consuming focus is positive, it is a Higher Power working in your life. A famous theologian considers God to be simply one's "Ultimate Concern." Your consuming interest is your god.

Acknowledge that your dependency is bigger than you, understand that it will take a power greater than you to help you turn yourself around, and turn the problems of your life over to your Higher Power.

EXERCISES

Jason finds that he misses and very much needs the faith of his childhood. He realizes that faith can be a powerful resource in his life and that it can provide him with the security and comfort he needs if he is to turn his life around. Is that sort of spiritual resource available to you?

A. Most people have had some involvement with religion while growing up. They may be angry with God, or have moved away from church involvement, but they basically have a fairly clear concept of God. If that description applies to you, try the following exercises. If not, if you do not believe in the God described by traditional religions, skip these exercises and try those in sets B or C.

Did you attend a church, synagogue, or temple as a child? _____

How about some other place of worship? _____

Was it important to you at the time? _____

How so? _____

_____

Can you remember much about it? Write what you remember.

_____

_____

Did you go because your parents forced you to?

_____

_____

Can you remember a specific time when you were forced to go?

_____

_____

Are you angry at your parents for making you go? Are you angry at God for having been made to go?

_____

_____

In terms of your spiritual life, and your being able to draw upon spiritual resources within you, answer these questions:

What was the bad news about your early religious experience? What were you taught that now works against you?

_____

_____

What was the good news about your early religious experience? What were you taught that now works in your favor?

_____

_____

Has your concept of God grown up with you, or do you still view God the way you did as a child?

_____

_____

What is your concept of God now? Describe God.

_____

_____

_____

_____

Is your God a personal God? Will your God assist you in your recovery?

_____

_____

Starting right now, what could you do to bring the power of your spirituality back into your life? Will you do it?

_____

_____

_____

If you are angry because of early religious training, might that anger left over from childhood be keeping you from a grown-up, more adult relationship with your God?

_____

Might you be feeling angry at God about things that have happened, or not happened, in your life?

_____

Who could you talk to about enriching your spiritual life?

_____

_____

B. Some people like Sylvia have spiritual ideas and beliefs which do not fit most religions. Some can attend churches without having to fight the words spoken there. Even though they don't share the theological beliefs, they can "see beyond" the language, and are able to join in the shared spirituality, activities, and support of church members.

To what extent does this apply to you?

_____

_____

If it does not, skip this section and move on to section C. If this does describe you, read on . . . .

If you are comfortable in religious groups, how could you benefit more from your association with the church, synagogue, or temple?

___ more contact with members

___ personal contact with leader

___ greater involvement with service

___ involvement with activities

___ special interest or worship groups

___ special projects

___ opportunities for service

___ specialized resources

___ key people you can turn to when things are difficult

How would you go about seeking these out?

_____

_____

Who might know more about the availability of these resources?

_____

_____

If you are not comfortable with a religious organization, what other spiritual resources have you explored?

___ self-help groups

___ service groups

___ yoga classes

___ Twelve-Step recovery groups

___ special spiritually-oriented individuals with whom you can connect

___ spiritually-oriented therapy groups

___ recovery and spiritual literature

Many people have found personal rituals or devotions helpful if practiced regularly. Whatever your beliefs, by incorporating a regular spiritual practice you can strengthen your spiritual self and provide yourself with power for change.

What do you think would work for you?

_____

_____

_____

How could you include such practices into your daily life?

_____

_____

_____

How can you begin to experiment with turning problems over to the spirit which you acknowledge?

_____

_____

_____

Who can you go to to talk about this?

_____

_____

_____

C. Some, like Kathy, are not ready for acknowledging any sort of spiritual power outside of themselves. When faced with a seemingly overwhelming problem, they often "cave-in" quickly to the same feelings of inadequacy and paralysis that you may be feeling.

If this describes you, you might try answering the following question:

Haven't you already turned over your own life to a power greater than yourself?

Think about your problem. Is it a habit, an addiction, or compulsive behavior? If you are using, you are turning your problems over to chemicals. If you are eating, you are turning your problems over to food. If you have the disease of relationship addiction, you are turning it over to others.

Try answering the question again:

To what, or to whom, have you been attempting to turn over your problems?

_____

_____

_____

If you don't believe in God or some other spiritual power, and you have been trying to turn over your problems to some lower power such as a compulsion or an addictive agent, you seem to have painted yourself into a corner. Your problem is bigger than you, but it's the only other game in town. Sounds pretty bleak.

But don't give up. Winston Churchill, who led his country through some of the worst moments of its history during the German bombardment of World War II, gave one of his most memorable speeches to a group of students about your age. He started softly but sternly, repeating one phrase over and over again, each time more loudly and forcefully than the last: *Never give up!*

Ponder this: you can open yourself to your *own* spirituality without accepting other's beliefs. You can let yourself trust in your *own* Higher Power, the spirit that is within you, without having to believe in the existence of an outside God. You can become an investigator of your own Higher Power instead of having to study the spiritual doctrines of others, You can learn to recognize the difference between your willfulness—which keeps you in bondage to your compulsion or addiction—and the quiet, life-sustaining power of your own Higher Self.

Spend some time getting acquainted with your Higher Self. Look over the suggestions in the previous two sections. Many of them can be adapted for those without theological beliefs. In particular, you might find that some of the following alternatives appeal to you:

___ self-help groups

___ service groups

___ yoga classes

___ Twelve-Step recovery groups

___ special spiritually-oriented individuals with whom you can connect

___ spiritually-oriented therapy groups

___ recovery and spiritual literature

Sometimes you may have to translate the language. When others say "God," you say "my Higher Self." Remind yourself that using the words God or Spirit serves the same function for others that "Higher Self" does for you. You are not giving anything away.

Another helpful strategy is to surround yourself with good people, not people who are into their lower selves, their compulsions, or addictions in order to cope. Stick with people who have tuned into their Higher Selves.

Remember your own vulnerability, however. Not having an external Higher Power can make your recovery much more risky. A major trap for those whose Higher Power is their Higher Self is the power of denial and self-deception. It is very easy to simply return to a variation of your old way of coping and be convinced that is an act of the Higher Self. The error consists in underestimating your own disease.

Check out your motives. One way is to ask yourself:

Why am I doing this? Is there any way that this could be simply my old problem resurfacing?

Another good way is to create a personal review process.

Develop several trusted friends who know how you operate; they know both your higher and lower sides. At preplanned intervals, sit down with your reviewers and get their opinion about your actions. The key to this is your choice of friends. If you pick people who will not be honest and confrontational, or people who will enable you and tell you what you want to hear, it won't work. You also have to listen to the feedback, and take it seriously. If you play games, cover up, or ignore their concerns, you will sabotage the process.

If you were to set up a personal review process, who could you use as reviewers?

_____   _____

_____   _____

_____   _____

As a final follow-up to Steps Two and Three, you should write a plan for engaging a Higher Power. This plan must be your own, although you might get some ideas from the preceding sections.

I will develop and deepen my relationship with a Higher Power by:

_____

_____

_____

I will utilize the following spiritual resources:

_____

_____

_____

I will consider the following people as spiritual guides, and I will turn to them when I need help:

_____

_____

_____

I will avoid the willfulness/denial trap by:

_____

_____

_____

4

Taking Inventory:
Steps Four Through Seven

Untreated, sores fester. They become infected and present a worse threat to the victim than the original wound. To heal the sore, the infection must be drained and exposed to air and sunlight. Medicine must be administered; but without holding up the wound to the light of day, without finding out just what kind of problem it is and how big it is, the healer would be unable to heal.

Steps Four through Seven comprise the heart and soul of the Twelve-Step program. Without honest self-appraisal we are doomed to self-deception and cover-ups. Our problems run deep and the habits we have formed will always tempt us. This is where we must come clean, admit what we have become, and prepare ourselves for healing self-examination. Step Four brings to light the type and size of our problem:

4. Make a searching and honest moral inventory of yourself.

This model of healing applies to wounds of the soul. Step Four asks us to hold our lives up to the air and sunlight a searching and honest moral inventory. Through this self-assessment we set the direction for our own treatment.

This kind of close self-scrutiny is difficult for anyone. It seems even harder for young people. Adolescence is a time of breaking away from your role as a child and establishing yourself as an independent adult. This process takes a long time and has a lot of false starts. As you develop the ability to decide for yourself, it is easy to become proud of your accomplishments and defensive about your weaknesses. It seems difficult to admit to vulnerability and weaknesses and still feel good about yourself. But do you feel good about yourself now? You may find, to your surprise, that an honest self-assessment provides more strength, more power, and better basis for feeling good about yourself than you can possibly imagine.

Sylvia, Jason, and Kathy have started on their paths to recovery. They must now begin their inventories, confronting their backgrounds and personal traits, weaknesses and strengths, wounds and offenses. Through this process they will come to know themselves better and begin their healing.

SYLVIA

"Good afternoon, Sylvia." Dr. Perez was so original. Sylvia was not in a good mood.

Sylvia smiled. "Hi."

"How are you feeling?"

Sylvia decided that they must give lectures in psychology school on how to be boring. "OK, pretty good."

"Really?"

"Sure, why not?" Now Sylvia was getting perturbed.

"You look quiet today, or maybe it's more like just into yourself."

"Look, Dr. Perez, things are not great, but OK. So I don't get gushy."

"So you cover up," observed Dr. Perez.

Sylvia rolled her eyes. It was only five minutes into their third session together. "What do you mean?"

"Sylvia, did it ever occur to you that you don't have to put on a happy face for me, or for anyone else for that matter? Have you ever thought that whatever it is that you are trying to hide isn't nearly as bad as the fact that you're hiding it?" Sylvia looked at Dr. Perez skeptically. Dr. Perez continued, "If you don't share yourself with others, how can they know what you need, or even who you are? If you hide yourself, you can't expect others to find you. Just what is it you're trying so hard to hide?"

This time Sylvia didn't say anything, but the tears in her eyes said a great deal.

▼ ▼ ▼

Sylvia wasn't sure whether to go on. She looked around the room. It was 8:00 P.M., the OA meeting was full tonight, and everyone was looking at her. The leader was also looking at her, waiting.

"This is an anniversary for me," she said. "I haven't gone on a food binge for one month." There was more, but she fought with herself whether or not to say it. "But I want to sometimes. So badly. I even hoard stuff to eat, and save it just in case things get too bad." It was so hard to say these things in public. "I must have seventy-five dollars in junk food in my closet." It sounded so horrible that she wished she could climb right out of her skin and jump into another life.

"What keeps you from eating it?" asked the leader.

"You know, I just can't stand all the hiding and lies anymore. I hide things from my mother. I actually plan my social life around where and when I can binge. It's so sick! My whole life feels like one big cover up."

No one spoke. Sylvia looked at their faces. Good grief! Looking back at her was someone she hadn't noticed before; one of the cheerleaders from school! Rosalie looked Sylvia in the eye and gave her a knowing, caring, and very accepting I've-been-there smile.

▼ ▼ ▼

A week later, Sylvia was back in Dr. Perez's office. "I've been working at not covering up. My first reflex is to lie, change things, or avoid people who know the truth. But what I'm learning is that the people I'm the most honest with are the ones with whom I feel the most comfortable."

"So you've been practicing?"

"Yeah. Experimenting. The great social experiment."

"And you have been experiencing some success?" asked Dr. Perez.

"Yes," smiled Sylvia.

"Let me ask you something, Sylvia. How do you get up the nerve to take those risks? It must be very frightening."

"It sure is. I just sort of take a second to sort things out, and then I think to myself 'The world needs me,' or sometimes I think 'The universe will make sure it's all right.'"

"It's a leap of faith," reflected Dr. Perez.

"Yes. When I just decide that there is a reason behind my pain and a purpose behind my getting well, I do better at telling it like it is. Then I find that things just seem to work out better."

Dr. Perez thought a moment. "It's almost like you have signed a contract with the universe: 'I'll be myself, and I'll trust that there is a reason for it.'"

"So far it seems to be working for me," added Sylvia.

"Even if other people might think you're crazy?" smiled Dr. Perez.

"I guess that's just going to have to be their problem," answered Sylvia.

JASON

"Look, Jason . . . " It was Tenesha, one of the two girls who had challenged him before. "You may think that just because you say that you're going to change, you really are, but I don't buy it. No way! You have to do more than just say it!"

Jason was steamed. He had been back in the hospital now for two weeks. He had been going to all the activities, earning points, and especially putting up with these two girls. "I don't know what you want from me!" he yelled. "To hell with both of you!" He got up and stormed out of the room. If this cost him points, then so what! It was worth the thirty minutes of TV to be able to fight back.

Back in his room he threw himself on his bed, shoes and all. "Damn!" he thought. "How many times have I done that? I hold back till I can't take it anymore and then I blow up." As he began to calm down, Jason thought back and replayed similar situations in his mind. He remembered what each had cost him. Lost friends, lost jobs, lost chances, all for sixty seconds of satisfaction. Once in a while it had been worth it, but most of the time it had brought him nothing but grief. "It's like a drug," he thought.

"So what about this time," he wondered. "It did feel good, but what's it really going to cost me? I doubt that Tenesha will quit bugging me. I lost points. I'm back where I started, so I lost two weeks." He rolled over. "I probably shouldn't have blown off," he thought. "No, I definitely shouldn't have. I wish I could re-run this one." He sat up. "Well, there's no way I can do it over, but I could take another run at it." Sighing, he rolled off the bed and headed back to the group.

"So, Jason . . . " the shrink began. This afternoon session had almost seemed too much to Jason, following his difficulties in the morning group. That, at least, had worked out OK. He made up his mind to listen this time and give the man a chance. "They tell me you've changed your attitude quite a bit since you went AWOL."

"Yeah, I guess I have."

"Any particular reason?"

"Sure," replied Jason. "If I'm going to get out of here and have a life, I've got to quit fighting it."

"So where did you learn you had to fight so much?" Jason hated it when shrinks turned an answer into an obvious question and then acted so smug about it.

"Fighting runs in our family."

"What did you do when your parents fought?"

"Acted normally," Jason thought to himself, "they were always fighting, anyway." "Kept out of the way, mostly," he answered. "The problem was when they were making up."

"How so?"

"They always expected me to act as if everything was fine and nothing had happened." Jason could remember both his parents smiling at him, looking like they had stomach pain they didn't want to admit to having.

"How did that make you feel?"

"I felt like hitting them, except that I felt like it would be wrong. Besides," he smiled, "my dad's kind of big."

"So, they expected you to act like they did," summarized the therapist, "make happy and act as if everything was fine when it wasn't."

"Right."

"And now?" the therapist prompted.

"What?"

"And now how are you feeling about them?"

"I don't know." answered Jason. "I hate them sometimes, and other times they're OK."

"How about now?" the therapist kept up.

Jason was quiet, but his face was turning red and the veins stood out in his neck.

"Do you think," the therapist gently asked, "that the pressure your parents put on you to conform might have something to do with your reaction to the girls in the group?"

▼ ▼ ▼

At dinner Jason sat across from Duvall. Duvall was grinning while Jason related the events of the morning and how Jason's anger at his parents had been spilling into the group and into the rest of his life.

"Those girls probably deserved it," laughed Duvall. "They have their own hang-ups."

Just then Tenesha walked by their table. She smiled and said "Hi" to Jason. Now he was really confused. How could she have been so confrontational at the meeting and so nice here?

Tenesha turned to Duvall. "So are you taking care of the new guy, Duvall?"

"Better believe it," Duvall smiled.

▼ ▼ ▼

Later that evening, Jason sat alone in the front pew of the small chapel. The quiet, the flowers on the altar, even the smell was comforting to him. He took several deep breaths and let the stillness sink in. Jason could feel the calming within. "God," Jason prayed, "help me overcome my weaknesses. Forgive me for all the hurt I have caused others."

KATHY

The bookstore was crowded with morning shoppers. It had that bookstore smell, and Kathy was browsing through the recovery section, killing time until Nicole's coffee break at 10:30. Kathy was impressed that Nicole had a job, and slightly envious. If only she could find a job.

Self-Help for Codependents. The title jumped out at her. She turned the book over and read the blurb on the back. "Hmm," she thought, "interesting." She flipped through the book, checking out the table of contents and sampling bits and pieces of the writing. Looking at the price, she decided to go ahead and get it.

"Hi!" It was Nicole. "What are you getting?"

Kathy showed her. "I'm going to try it for a while."

"You know," said Nicole, "you are really working hard. I'm impressed. It's been three weeks now, and you're still hanging in there."

Kathy smiled. "You and your family have been so good to me. It's time for me to be contributing. I wanted to talk to you about finding work."

"Let's sit down." They went outside and sat on the bench in front of the store. "Where have you looked?"

"I thought about being a waitress. I could probably get a job at the Peppermill, but I think I'd like something more interesting."

"Such as?"

"I don't know . . . " Kathy paused. "I've watched you at your job. You talk about new books that have come out. I like being in the bookstore. Do you think they might be hiring soon?"

"You know what," Nicole brightened, "I think Jim is giving notice this week. I'll bet the manager will be looking to replace him. I'll talk to her about it."

"Thanks, Nicole. Listen, I know you need to get back to work—I'll see you at dinner. Don't forget, we've got the meeting tonight."

▼ ▼ ▼

Working through the recovery book that afternoon had been fairly easy. There wasn't much text, and it was relatively short. At least until now. It was almost dinnertime, and she had gotten into a section on past hurts. While filling out a chart, she had to write down any experiences during which she had been sexually abused.

At first she just blew it off and went on. Then something stopped her, and she sat quietly, scarcely daring to breathe. Images floated back. Kathy knew she didn't want to think about it, to remember, but it had always been there. Her stepfather had hardly waited until he had unpacked after the wedding before he had been in her room. Shutting it in the back of her mind, Kathy made a few notes on the page, and closed the book. She would come back to it later.

▼ ▼ ▼

The meeting had started on time, and after the formalities the discussion had centered upon victimization.

"Many of us were victimized as children," began the speaker. "Some of us were hurt physically, some mentally, some sexually. And when we were victimized, we learned several bad things." Kathy looked down.

She thought about her own experiences. I've never told anyone. Someday . . . .

The speaker continued. "One thing we often come to believe is that we deserved the abuse, or that we don't deserve better. We do not feel we are really worthwhile. We believe that we must earn others' love. In my life I am always trying to please others."

"Wow," thought Kathy, "a people-pleaser too. I've been one all my life."

The speaker went on to list a number of other behavior patterns that follow from sexual abuse. Kathy felt like her life was being laid out for all to see. Then the speaker talked about the ways victims can turn out to be abusers themselves. "We end up hurting others because we are in such pain," she went on. "Because I was hurt I find myself unable to stop hurting others, even though I don't want to. I have ended up poisoning relationship after relationship. My greatest shame is what I have done to my children."

On the way home Kathy and Nicole were quiet. Kathy thought about the workbook sections she had hurried through so quickly that afternoon. "Maybe I'll go back and do them over," she thought.

▼ ▼ ▼

They sat together at the kitchen table. It was after 11:00 P.M. Kathy spoke. "You must be tired, Nicole. You have that early class tomorrow, and then you work in the afternoon. You ought to get some sleep."

"Yeah, it is tiring, but you know what? I've really been enjoying talking to you lately. Even this late." Nicole's fatigue showed in her eyes, but she looked intent. "What did you think about the speaker?"

Kathy paused and thought for a while. Nicole sipped her coffee and did not push. Finally Kathy reached an inner decision. "When I was eleven my stepfather did things to me. Sexual things, which I am ashamed of." She looked down. "I couldn't tell my mother, or anyone else."

"I'm terribly sorry . . . " started Nicole.

Kathy's eyes watered. "I was afraid that if I told anyone, they wouldn't want to be near me."

Nicole remained quiet.

Kathy started again. "I've been thinking about that speaker a lot. I've been wondering about how I come across to people. I'm kind of an obnoxious person, aren't I?"

"You haven't been lately," replied Nicole.

"I mean before."

"You always seemed so desperate. You would do or say anything to get attention."

"Looking back, it seems so stupid. But even now I sometimes want to say something that will stop people right in their tracks. Other times I want to get in their face and make sure they know I'm alive."

"It sounds pretty lonely," offered Nicole.

Kathy looked at her. "I'm terrified that I will never have friends or be loved. I have this horrible nightmare every now and then. I'm standing in the middle of the desert, on this dry lake bed. The sky is an empty blue and the light is intense. My parents and friends are all getting in a car and driving away, leaving me so alone." She thought some more. "I guess the things I do to get people to like me just end up driving them away. And I can't help it. I see myself doing something totally stupid and it's like I still can't stop."

"And all you end up doing . . . " Nicole paused.

" . . . is offending people and putting them off," finished Kathy.

They were both quiet for a while.

"You seem ready to quit. You've already started to stop your old behaviors." said Nicole.

"Yeah, I have. With your help, and the help of the part of me which can see through it all, I will."

Nicole smiled at Kathy. Then she thought of something. "By the way," she said. "I found another workbook you might be interested in." She reached over to the counter and pulled a book out of her bag.

Kathy looked at the title: *Dealing with Sexual Abuse.*

INSIGHTS

The first step in turning yourself around is admission: admitting you have a problem and that you need turning around. The second step is recognizing that the problem is bigger than you are and that you need help. The third step involves turning your will and life over to the care of a Higher Power. Now the next step is to ask just how big the problem really is. Sylvia, Jason, and Kathy are making some serious moves toward their recovery. They are now taking inventory. They are sizing up the problems they have, the personal characteristics which helped create their problems, and the hurt their problems have caused others.

An inventory is simply the process of adding up what you have and figuring out what you need. Stores conduct inventories all the time. They need to see what's selling and what isn't so they can make good business decisions. A personal inventory tells us how we are doing with our own lives, what things need to be changed, and what resources we have with which to work.

An inventory can help us understand why we do the things we do. It can assist us in recognizing when our problem cycle is self-destructive. It helps us confront our own denial and cover-ups. It allows us to understand and admit the pain we have caused others. This confession reduces our sense of guilt. We are brought back into harmony with the world, with others around us, and with ourselves.

How do you do such an inventory? It isn't easy, but it is straightforward. You ask yourself some important questions, think about them long and hard, and answer them as seriously and honestly as you can. Remember the introduction to this book? It has a paragraph which you should reread:

> However you use this book, use it honestly. There is no way this book, or any program, can help you if you are not honest. This may be a problem for you, or for anyone whose life needs to be turned around. Part of the difficulty of dealing with problems is that we are all human. This means that we do the best we can to survive. In order to overcome our difficulties, we learn to minimize them, to ignore our own complaints. We deny the size of the problem.

We must start with describing, in as much detail as we can, the things we are doing that have gotten us in trouble. Much of this has already been done in Chapter Two. We must go further, however, and look at the way in which our problem behavior has served to only make things worse for us and how our attempts to correct it have failed in the past.

Loss figures heavily in our attempts to turn around. As a result of our desperate actions we lose friends, property, respect from others and ourselves, and even our own identity. In making the necessary changes we fear even more losses, especially the one we have been relying upon the most lately: our problem. These real and anticipated losses must be tallied. We must confront the ways we deny and cover up our problems. Our powers of deception are immense, and we need to be vigilant.

*E*XERCISES

Because we so easily deceive ourselves into believing the best or worst, someone else's opinion can be helpful. Not just anyone's, however—opinions are only as good as their sources. Think about the people in your life. Some don't really know you, and some have problems worse than yours. Whose opinion could you really trust?

Name	*Phone or location*
_____	_____
_____	_____
_____	_____
_____	_____

Call these people feedback sources, because they will feed their reactions back to you about whether or not they feel your answers are honest and accurate. Caution! Do not pick someone who has the same problem you are trying to overcome! They may not be in any better position than you to be objective. If you are in a recovery program that includes a "sponsor," then he or she may be the best person to fulfill this role.

After working through the exercises in this section, consider asking your feedback sources to review your answers with you. This may be hard. You have to let them know how important it is that they be honest, even if it means hurting your feelings.

Also, because taking on this challenge is very difficult, you will need support in your efforts. You or your feedback sources may be discussing things that are painful. You will need someone else to talk to who can listen to you when you are tired, depressed, or angry. Who could give you that kind of support?

Name   *Phone or location*

_____   _____

_____   _____

_____   _____

_____   _____

Before going much further, it would be a good idea to contact these people and get them to agree to help in those ways.

*P*roblem Cycles

Problems run in cycles. Something triggers the cycle, the problem behavior takes over, and the situation gets worse. This happens in two ways. Using the problem behavior to cope, Sylvia, Jason, and Kathy made things worse than they were before. The coping behavior provided temporary relief from the immediate stress but increased stress in the long run. But even worse, Sylvia, Jason, and Kathy never learned to handle the difficult situation in the first place.

Use the following questions to see if your problem is circular. Visualize again the last few times the problem occurred.

Were others around? Who?

_____

_____

What were they doing?

_____

_____

_____

How might their actions have been affecting you?

_____

_____

How did you interpret the situation at the time?

_____

_____

What sort of messages were you giving yourself?

_____

_____

How were you feeling by this time?

_____

_____

As a result of the situation and your inner reactions to it, what sort of things did you actually do?

_____

_____

Did your actions then make the situation better or worse?

_____

_____

Has this way of dealing with situations become a problem?

_____

_____

What have been the long-range effects of dealing with things in this way?

_____

_____

*T*rying to Change

You have probably already decided that things are not working for you or you would not have gotten this far along in this book. And you have probably also decided to quit doing what you're doing—perhaps several times by now! What you first used to make the situation better has itself become a bigger problem than you had before.

To what extent has this temporary solution become a problem?

_____

_____

Think about each time you tried to change your problem behavior in the past. Did you try the same method each time? Did you use any special techniques? Were you involved in any programs?

_____

_____

_____

What have you tried so far to solve this problem?

_____

_____

How did it work?

_____

_____

What goes wrong with your attempts to change?

_____

_____

*W*hat Keeps You There?

There are probably forces at work that you don't fully understand which are keeping you from change. Let's think through some of them.

We keep following the same old patterns, making the same old mistakes, and giving the same lame excuses to ourselves because we haven't found new answers. Usually we find ourselves getting into trouble because of a vulnerability.

It may be a lack of self-confidence, a belief that we will always fail, or an assumption that no one will really like us. Or it could be something more complicated. We may have a need to get hurt to punish ourselves, or to get back at someone else. Or perhaps we feel pushed to rewrite history, to conquer some dead-end situation which defeated us in the past. This is a shortcoming. It keeps us from changing in ways that would make our lives better. We keep playing out a losing script.

Such weaknesses and defects can be caused by past hurts or current circumstances. They can shape our futures, however, because they shape our expectations. And expectations shape how we experience and how we respond to things. Expectations are like audio cassettes. You get in a particular kind of situation, and they slip in and play. The music they play determines how you dance. In this case, how you think shapes what you get.

Are you in tune yet with some of the past experiences which might have shaped your current expectations?

Write some of them down:

Experience (what happened)

1. _____
2. _____
3. _____
4. _____

Expectation (what you "learned to expect" from it)

1. _____
2. _____
3. _____
4. _____

58

Sometimes expectations are triggered by being in certain places. If you had bad experiences in school as a child, it is quite possible that you now feel uncomfortable and defensive in school settings. This could be because the school setting reminds you of the difficulties in the past, and so triggers off expectations that the present situation is also going to create discomfort and hurt.

Expectations can hurt in three ways. First, others' expectations of you can limit you. Acting on their expectations, they can pressure you into your problem behavior or they can prevent you from showing them wrong. But others' expectations aren't the most damaging. Yours are! Your expectations of yourself can limit you—

▼ If you feel that you will fail, you probably will.

▼ If you feel that the only way you can cope is to engage in your problem behavior, you probably will.

—and your expectations of others can limit you:

▼ If you feel others won't like you, you probably will act in unlikable ways.

▼ If you expect that others will hurt you or let you down, you probably will not give them a chance to prove you wrong.

Second, the company you keep can keep you from changing. It is when you are faltering that you need to surround yourself with people who can help you make it, not people who will help you fail again. When you are weak, and you are ready to toss in the towel and take a drink, or cut class, or get in a fight, or whatever it is that you want to do, that is *not* the time to have a "friend" come up and say, "What the hay, let's do it!"

Think about your friends. Be honest with yourself! Which of your friends are good for you and which ones feed your problem?

Good friends:

_____   _____

_____   _____

_____   _____

_____   _____

Enablers (the ones who make it easy for you to get into your problem cycle):

_____   _____

_____   _____

_____   _____

_____   _____

The final thing that keeps you from changing is dependency. There are two kinds of dependency. One is physical dependency. If you have been using substances like alcohol or drugs you may be physically dependent. This means that your efforts to quit will create physical cravings for the substance. Some people can break a physical dependency "cold turkey," but it is difficult and often requires medical assistance.

__ Do you have a physical dependency?

__ Does your substance use "get you back to normal" instead of getting you high like it used to?

__ Have you stopped getting high to party and started partying to get high?

__ Is your use of drugs and/or alcohol starting to interfere with other parts of your life?

__ Have you been told by friends, teachers, or employers that you have changed?

__ Have you changed social groups, from the people you knew to a more tolerant group?

The other kind of dependency is psychological. This one can be worse. We become psychologically addicted to using, to abusing food, to cutting classes, to running away, or to any of the other problem behaviors because they help us cope. Physical dependencies are difficult to break in the short run, but psychological dependencies are harder in the long run. Many people complete a thirty-day dependency recovery program, suffer through withdrawal, get clean, and then go back to their addiction because they could not cope psychologically without using.

If you want to change yourself and turn your life around, you are going to have to change the influences around you. You are going to have to challenge your own expectations and become aware of when you are setting yourself up for defeat. You are going to have to take your dependencies seriously and not act upon them. They will not go away by themselves. And finally, you are going to have to sort through your friends and get rid of the deadwood that drags you down. Friends who help destroy you are worse than no friends at all.

*E*asy Answers That Cost a Lot

Some problems are circular because each stage is part of a cycle. When the cycle is up we feel good, and want to stay on it. When it is down we feel bad, and want to go up again. Each stage leads to the next, and so the cycle tends to perpetuate itself. Yet something powers it, or it would just fizzle out. The cycle is powered by investment. Just as we take care of things we pay a lot for, we protect those things in which we have invested much time and energy, and from which we benefit. In order to break a problem cycle it is first necessary to find out what we gain from it, then find better ways to get those benefits.

Perhaps by drinking, you are able to reduce anxiety. Perhaps by starting family fights you are able to avoid making difficult changes in the relationships. Perhaps by putting off difficult assignments you are able to get out of being judged by others.

Take a few minutes (or a few days!) to think about what you have to gain by not changing. What's in it for you to continue the cycle you get into? It's often hard to look at our own motives in this way, but try to imagine you are a detective investigating yourself.

Start by looking at the overall problem you have decided to overcome: what sorts of gains might you have been enjoying as a result of your problem behavior? Check those which apply:

__ a quick "rush" or "high"?

__ avoiding something worse?

__ dealing with difficult feelings?

__ avoiding some challenge?

__ sending a message?

__ controlling some other person?

__ denying a painful change?

__ controlling fear or anxiety?

__ avoiding a serious risk?

__ putting off taking care of some other business?

__ having a sense of at least some control in difficult situations?

__ living out someone else's idea of how you should be?

__ something else? What? _____

_____

The gains you have checked can give you some interesting information. Have you ever wondered why you need these particular gains? If your problem behavior is drinking, for instance, and if you checked "a quick rush," "controlling anxiety," and "some control in a difficult situation," then you can look at those gains and figure out what underlying needs you have. If you desire a quick rush then you seem to need some sort of escape or excitement in your life. If you desire to control anxiety then you probably need a greater sense of security. If you desire control then you apparently need a greater sense of power. Translate those gains into the needs which they meet:

I need _____

I need _____

I need _____

Sometimes it's hard to figure out why we keep doing something that is bad for us. Usually it's because we are getting something out of doing it. This is called "secondary gain." Secondary gain is often difficult to identify because the cycle of undesirable behavior seems so damaging and the gain seems so small. Other times it is hard to understand because the gain is complicated.

*L*osses

Your problem has caused you grief. You may have lost friends, money, jobs, or personal property through your mismanagement or need to feed your habit. Let's take inventory of those losses.

As a result of your problem, have you lost money? _____

When?	How much?	How?
_____	_____	_____
_____	_____	_____
_____	_____	_____

As a result of your problem, have you lost property? _____

When?	How much?	How?
_____	_____	_____
_____	_____	_____
_____	_____	_____

How much money or property in all would you estimate that you have lost because of your problem? _____

_____

At this rate, how much do you stand to lose in the future, if you don't turn things around?

_____

As a result of your problem, have you lost friends? _____

Who?	Why?
_____	_____
_____	_____
_____	_____

Who are your friends now?

_____	_____
_____	_____
_____	_____

Would they still be your friends if you turned your problem around? Will they support your efforts at recovery? Be realistic; this question is very important.

_____

_____

Which friends will undermine and work against your recovery?

_____	_____
_____	_____
_____	_____

As a result of your problem, have you ever lost control? _____

Incident	Result
_____	_____
_____	_____
_____	_____

How much control do you now have over yourself when you engage in your problem behavior?

_____

At what point do you start to lose control when you engage in your problem behavior?

_____

Typically, what happens when you lose control of yourself?

_____

_____

As a result of your problem, have you lost respect? _____

Whose respect meant the most to you prior to your involvement in problem behavior?

_____

_____

How do they feel about you now?

_____

_____

Have you lost respect from those whose respect you value?

_____

_____

Whose respect have you lost?

_____	_____
_____	_____

How much did their respect mean to you?

_____

_____

Could you earn their respect back? What would you have to do to
earn it back?

_____

_____

To what extent have you lost your self-respect?

_____

_____

What would you have to do to earn it back?

_____

_____

As a result of your problem, have you lost your sense of identity?

_____

How have you changed since your problem behavior began?

_____

_____

Are you doing things you don't want to be doing? What?

_____

_____

How have you ended up compromising values which you hold?

_____

_____

Are you becoming someone you do not want to be?

_____

_____

Could you discover who you really are while continuing your problem behavior? Why or why not?

_____

_____

What changes would it take for you to discover who you really are?

_____

_____

_____

Cover ups

Denial was a particularly important problem for Jason. His denial, along with his anger, kept him from benefiting from his recovery program. He ran away from Haven House and from conflicts with other patients. But this pattern of running is nothing new to him. He had been running into a bottle and hiding there for some time. Facing up to things directly was Jason's biggest move toward recovery, and he is still in the process of facing up to his problems.

In order to maintain our problem cycle (whether it is an addiction, compulsion, or other behavior) we often cover up, hiding our behavior from others as well as from ourselves. We do this so we won't get caught, won't be confronted, won't have to change.

Which cover-up strategies do you now use? Circle those that apply.

hiding evidence	lying	cover stories
explanations	justifications	rationalization
alibi	blaming	denial
displaced anger	smokescreens	exaggeration
minimization	stealing	

other: _____

Even if these were really working, the effect would only be to keep you malfunctioning. But they might not even be working as well as you think. A great many people might be seeing right through your attempts, and your problem might already have gone public.

*S*hame

Deception is demeaning. We are embarrassed by our problems and by our attempts to cover them up. As a result of losing self-control and self-respect and using lies and deception to cover-up, we often end up harboring deep feelings of shame. As our lives become less and less manageable, we become more and more embarrassed. Our dignity is compromised.

How bad is the shame that you feel? If you were to rate the degree of shame you feel on a ten point scale, how would you rate it?

Check the appropriate place:

L_____	_____	_____	_____	_____
0	2	4	6	8	10
shame-free		moderate shame		extreme shame	

What would you have to change in your life to be able to overcome the shame you feel now, and to live shame-free?

_____

_____

*P*ain We Have Caused Others

Our problem behavior can hurt more than just ourselves. Through our misguided attempts at coping and our subsequent cover-ups, it is quite likely that we have hurt those around us. It isn't just our actual actions that can hurt. We can hurt with our attitudes. We convey our beliefs and moods by the look in our eye, the way we hold ourselves, and the words we choose. Finally, we can hurt ourselves and others by the way we are. If we are unforgiving, rigid, or defensive, we set up hurtful situations that prevent our recovery.

The following are personal traits that make recovery difficult and may be hurtful to others. Circle those which apply to you.

helplessness	explosiveness	dishonesty
defensiveness	impatience	rage
impulsiveness	distrust	destructiveness
irresponsibility	fear	jealousy
perfectionism	false pride	false humility

others: _____

Of the above, the three most hurtful are probably:

_____ _____ _____

Who could you go to to check that out? _____

It is quite normal to have negative feelings. Having negative *attitudes* is different, however. Attitudes are persistent and enduring, and they shape how we see and respond to others.

The following abusive attitudes can make recovery difficult and can be hurtful to others. Circle those which apply.

resentful	contemptuous	paranoid
arrogant	pessimistic	intolerant
patronizing	critical	skeptical
envious	judgmental	moralistic
distrustful	self-centered	unforgiving
aloof	punitive	shaming

Attitudes are often difficult to see in ourselves. Would the same person you just mentioned be the best one with whom to check out your perceptions about your attitudes?

If not, then who? _____

List specific actions you have taken which have caused hurt, bitterness, fear, resentment, or separation. Specify what happened, the part you played, and who suffered. To indicate when it happened, given an approximate date or time frame ("November, 1983" or "when I was 13").

When _____

What happened _____

_____

_____

The part you played _____

_____

_____

Who suffered _____

_____

. . . .

When _____

What happened _____

_____

_____

The part you played _____

_____

_____

Who suffered _____

_____

. . . .

When _____

What happened _____

_____

_____

The part you played _____

_____

_____

Who suffered _____

_____

69

*P*ersonal Resources

So far this has been a process of listing the bad news only. It would be unfair and inaccurate to leave it at this. Everyone has a good side as well. Here is an opportunity to highlight some of your good traits, attitudes, and actions. These will prove to be the strengths and resources you can draw on in turning yourself around.

Circle those which apply to you.

strength	honesty	openness
patience	trust	inner calmness
reliability	responsibility	constructiveness
courage	tolerance	perspective
self-pride	true humility	

other: _____

Of these, my three strongest traits are probably:

_____ _____ _____

Who could you go to to check this out? _____

The following constructive attitudes can make recovery easier, can help in overcoming obstacles, and can strengthen your relationship with others. Circle those which apply.

concern	love	willingness
humility	optimism	openness
support	tolerance	assistance
belief	appreciation	acceptance
moral sense	integrity	trust
other-centeredness	forgiveness	directness

Would the same person you just mentioned be the best one with whom to check out your attitudes? _____

Decide in advance whether you are willing to take that person's opinions seriously—we all have a tendency to discount positive feedback.

If not that person, then who? _____

Think back over your actions in the past. Have you done anything of which you are particularly proud? Did you excel at something, help someone when they needed it, or accomplish something difficult? Have you proven yourself to be reliable and trustworthy in the past? Have you ever done something hard just because it was the right thing to do?

List specific actions you have taken which have been helpful to others or enhanced your life:

When _____

What I did _____

_____

Who benefited _____

_____

. . . .

When _____

What I did _____

_____

Who benefited _____

_____

. . . .

When _____

What I did _____

_____

Who benefited _____

_____

. . . .

Confiding in others

We must continue the admissions process by acknowledging the ways that we have hurt others.

Step Five focuses upon this:

5. Admit to your Higher Power, yourself, and to another human being the exact nature of your limitations.

Have you been sharing your work on this chapter with a feedback source? Step five requires that we share the nature of our wrongs with someone else. If you did not pick a feedback source, it is important for you to choose someone now with whom you can share what you have written in this chapter.

The person you select could be a close friend or someone you barely know. It could be someone your own age, or it could be an adult. Whoever it is, you need to spend enough time with him or her to go over your answers in detail.

List several possible people below:

Name   *Phone or location*

_____   _____

_____   _____

_____   _____

_____   _____

Choose one of these people and make contact. Do not wait or allow yourself to talk yourself out of it. Do not go on with these exercises until you have made contact.

*R*eadiness

If you undertake an honest and searching moral inventory, you can explore the ways you have caused hurt to others, resulting in resentment, fear, bitterness, and perhaps even separation. You can better understand how you have manipulated those around you, been dishonest and selfish, and allowed anger and bad feelings to spoil your most important relationships. You must prepare yourself to overcome the factors which have created pain in your life and the lives of those around you. This is the purpose of Step Six:

6. Prepare to have your Higher Power remove all of your limitations.

Step Six asks you to ready yourself to have God or your Higher Power remove all of those limitations that have brought on your problem, helped maintain it, or hurt others through it.

Review the list of secondary gains you compiled on p. 61. Rewrite them here.

_____

_____

_____

_____

_____

These are the things you stand to lose by turning yourself around.

Review the alternative ways you have of satisfying these needs, which you listed on p. 70. Rewrite them here.

_____

_____

_____

_____

These are ways to minimize the losses you stand to suffer by the changes you are attempting to make.

Review the losses you have already suffered as a result of *not* turning yourself around which you compiled on pages 62–66.

money _____

property _____

friends _____

control _____

respect _____

identity _____

Review the losses you believe you will continue to suffer if you do not change (which you listed following each specific loss in the loss section on pages 62–66). How bad might things get?

money _____

property _____

friends _____

control _____

respect _____

identity _____

Look over the answers you have written in this section. If you choose to change, you will live with one set of consequences. If you choose not to change, you will live with another set of consequences. It's your choice. The ball is now in your court.

THE SEVENTH STEP

One final piece of business remains in this section. Step Six asked you to prepare yourself to "have your Higher Power remove all of your limitations." All the shortcomings of your life—your problem behavior, your personal traits and attitudes leading up to your problem, your inability to put things right in your life—you must be ready to let them go. Step Seven then requires you to

7. Humbly ask your Higher Power to remove all of your limitations.

Letting go of your problem behavior requires humility. You must be strong enough to admit that your attempts to control your stressful world with your problem behavior have failed. You must let go of your false pride and willfulness long enough to accept every bit of assistance you can find. This means recognizing that calling upon your Higher Power is critical. However you think about this Higher Power, whatever relationship you feel you have with your Higher Power, now is the time to use that power to save your life.

If you are, in fact, ready to give up your various shortcomings, and you do believe in a personal Higher Power who can exercise that sort of direct effect in your life, your work is clear. You must give yourself over in faith and trust to allow your Higher Power to assist you.

Are you still having trouble with the notion of a Higher Power? Does the entire process bog down for you when you come up against the notion of a personal God being necessary to your recovery? What if you simply do not believe in such a God? Are you then bound to suffer forever?

There are several ways of interpreting Steps Six and Seven. Perhaps this outline of different ways of looking at spiritual matters would help.

For Jason to complete Steps Six and Seven, he must open his heart in prayer to allow God's power to assist him in his struggle. Jason must give up trying to control his own life and let the divine power of God take over. By allowing God to work through him, Jason will empower himself.

Because Sylvia's Higher Power is the power and direction of the universe itself, she must bring herself spiritually in line with the greater world. She must move beyond her own petty wants and concerns, and find what the world has in store for her. Sylvia believes that the purpose and mission of her life is the same as that of the universe. Therefore she must find a way to live in accordance with the physical and spiritual universe. She must humbly ask the universe to remove her shortcomings.

For Kathy to complete Steps Six and Seven, she must give herself over to the direction set by her own Higher Self. She must ready herself to give up the old patterns which brought her grief, and trust that her Higher Self has the wisdom and power necessary to combat self-deception and despair. Kathy must learn to separate the directions set by the Higher Self from the manipulations of her lower self. She must draw the power, wisdom, and direction from her Higher Self into the here and now.

Just as Jason, Sylvia, and Kathy each require a different approach to complete Steps Six and Seven, depending upon his or her own unique spirituality, so will you.

Given the Higher Power that you acknowledge, what must you do to prepare yourself so that your shortcomings can be removed?

_____

_____

_____

In what manner can you communicate with your Higher Power? How could you convey your readiness and need to your Higher Power?

_____

_____

_____

What is your plan for doing this?

_____

_____

_____

TARGETS FOR DEEPER WORK

In taking stock of themselves, Jason, Sylvia, and Kathy discovered that they each had undergone special hurt or were dealing with special situations. Sylvia had suffered terrible loss and learned that she needed to finish her grieving before she could completely gain control of her anxiety-induced food binges. Kathy learned that her relationship addiction could be related to past sexual trauma. Jason had to cope with a family situation which would actively work against his recovery. They each have more work to do in these areas. If you need further work on one of these problems, the next three sections are for you. Chapter Five focuses upon past hurts and traumas. Chapter Six deals with resolving early losses. Finally, Chapter Seven explores how to deal with problem families.

You are invited to work on any of these three chapters, as they apply to you. If none of them apply, however, you may skip directly to Chapter Eight.

5

Letting Go of Past Hurts
or Traumas

This chapter is for you if you have undergone traumatic events in your life. It is designed to help you work through painful memories and come to understand the way in which that trauma helped lead you to your problem behavior and helps maintain it as well. If you have not experienced trauma, then you may skip this chapter and move ahead. But before you do, you might want to look it over and see if there is any past hurt in your life that you want to address.

KATHY

A night breeze rustled the leaves outside Kathy's window. It was after midnight, but Kathy was working. She sat at her desk, reading the workbook Nicole had give her earlier that evening. As instructed, she had several pencils and some extra paper ready. "My gosh," she thought, "I can't believe I'm doing this."

She had been avoiding this moment for nearly ten years. At the time there had been fear. Her stepfather (she still couldn't bring herself to even think his name) had threatened her into silence. Later she had been paralyzed by shame. She felt responsible for what had occurred and responsible for protecting her mother's feelings. Recently, it had been more that she feared being kicked out of her mother's life for rocking the boat and being rejected by the kids at school if they ever found out. It had also been a long time, and it simply seemed easier to ignore the whole thing, as if it were a bad dream, than to drag it all out and remember. Kathy was afraid of the memories.

With resolve matched only by the uncertainty she felt, Kathy wrote her name in the space provided. "There," she thought, "I've done it."

The first section talked about how reading and working through a book like this could be difficult. Kathy could believe that easily enough. It explained how dealing with painful memories could be overwhelming and cause distress. The book suggested that the reader locate several people who were trustworthy and tell them about the book. Those people could be asked to serve as listeners and to provide support and perspective as needed. The book went on to say that since the memories and questions the book might stir up could be powerful and overwhelming, it was preferable to use the book under a therapist's care. "At least," it went on to say, "locate a therapist whom you would be comfortable contacting should your reactions be so strong that you need professional assistance to get through them."

"Good grief," thought Kathy. "Do I really want to go through with this? Am I setting myself up to get hurt? Wouldn't it be easier to close this thing right now and walk away?" The breeze stirred the leaves outside her window again. Kathy turned the page and read on.

▼ ▼ ▼

Nicole had been enthusiastic about being a listener for Kathy and had offered her the name of one of her other friends who Nicole thought would also be a good listener. Kathy had met Denise over coffee and had liked her immediately. Denise had agreed, suggesting that they meet together occasionally and share experiences. Today they were sitting at a restaurant having lunch.

"Kathy, Nicole told me about your program," Denise began. "I'm impressed. How can I help?"

"Thanks. I'm working through a workbook about my background. I was abused by my stepfather. The book said that I might go through some difficult times while I deal with it, and having someone to talk it over with could help."

Denise was intent. "I went through something similar, and it does help. I've found that the more people I talk to, the easier it is. I'd appreciate being able to talk with you about it. Let's do it."

"One other thing," said Kathy, "the book said I should think about finding a counselor or someone to turn to if things got out of hand.

What do you think?"

"It may not get that bad, but I do know someone, just in case. He works for Community Mental Health, so he's not expensive. I've gone a couple of times."

"Do you trust him?" asked Kathy.

"Yes, I do. I went when things were tough, and he helped me make connections and understand things I wasn't seeing on my own."

"Do you think I need to go into therapy?"

"I don't know you that well," replied Denise, "but you know where to find him if you need to. Why don't we think about what would make you want to see a therapist. I've got a piece of paper, so we can write them down. What sorts of things would have to be going wrong before you would consider going?"

▼ ▼ ▼

Kathy was back at her desk. The questions were harder now. She had been asked to describe her abuse, focusing upon one incident. She struggled with it. She had known going in that it would be demanding, and it was. The images that came and went were disturbing, and when she tried to put them into words she drew blanks. From time to time she would distract herself by eating, going to the bathroom, thinking about other things, or contemplating sleep. Yet she persisted.

Then she remembered the first time. She had heard him enter the room in the dark. She could tell it was him because the bed sank to one side when he sat on it. He hadn't said much. She remembered how rough his hands were, and how his breath smelled of alcohol. She remembered his weight and how uncomfortable and confused she was, but not much more. Except that he had said, "This is our secret. If you tell your mother, it will hurt her a lot. She won't love you anymore, and you'll have to go live in a foster home."

Following the book's directions, she started by writing down just what she had seen. That was easy, because it had been dark. Vague shapes and shadows. She remembered watching the streetlight shine through the window and fall on the bedspread. Then she remembered seeing him on the bed, in his bathrobe. That memory made her shudder.

Then Kathy focused on sounds. She could hear the "click" of the door latch as it opened. She could hear the way he had talked to her.

79

That sound made her stomach churn, and she was overcome by a sinking feeling. It took her ten minutes to pull her strength together and get back to writing.

She tried to remember the physical sensations, but that was harder. She remembered the roughness of his hands. "Funny," she thought, "no emotional reaction." She recalled his pressing weight upon her. Sitting at her desk, Kathy had trouble breathing. As she wrote about the feeling of being pressed down, she found herself taking sudden deep breaths as if to reassure herself that she could still breathe. "I wonder," she thought, "if that has anything to do with how upset I get when boys put their arms over my shoulders when we're walking?"

The writing became easier. Remembered sensations became images, images turned to words. Words led to sentences. After a while Kathy looked up. She had been writing nonstop for over an hour.

As she wrote she felt herself coming nearer and nearer to understanding something. It wasn't so much the physical pain. Not even the feeling of being intimidated, controlled, and used. The abuse had been bad, but there was something much worse which had pulled the rug right out from under her as a person. Finally it came clear. Her stepfather had been awful, but it was her mother who had hurt her the worst. Kathy now had the connection she needed: when she *had* told her mother, her mother had not believed her. She had denied Kathy's reports of abuse; she had minimized and ignored them. And for a reason. She had not wanted Kathy to come between her and her new husband. She had betrayed her daughter's trust and well-being to protect her marriage. Kathy had been sold out.

▼ ▼ ▼

Kathy tossed in her sleep. It was happening all over again. The door latch clicked, the shadowy figure approached and sat down on her bed. Rough hands gave way to the oppressive weight. Kathy couldn't breathe. She fought for breath and started to scream. This time she shouted "Stop!"

The dream changed. It was the empty, dry lake bed. The deep blue sky was cloudless and the distant mountains shimmered in the heat. She was alone. Kathy turned and saw the long black car. Her mother and stepfather were climbing in to drive away and leave her. This time Kathy was not panicked. She was not terrified of the coming isolation. This time she was angry. Furiously she ran to the car, reaching it before the door closed. Yanking it open, she dragged her stepfather out of the car, pummeling him with her fists. He struggled to his feet and started running away across the lake bed. She turned to face her mother . . . .

▼ ▼ ▼

As the early morning light spilled through the window and across the kitchen table, Nicole found Kathy sipping coffee. "Good morning. You're up early."

"Hi," replied Kathy. She looked thoughtful. "You know what, Nicole?"

"What?"

"I've been thinking. I've been crazy for a long time."

"What do you mean?" asked Nicole.

"I've been hurt, angry, and frantic for so long, I've forgotten what 'normal' looks like." Nicole smiled. Kathy continued, "I've been running for a long, long time."

"From . . . " prompted Nicole.

"From my stepfather, Frank," replied Kathy.

"Frank?"

"That's his name. From him and what he did to me. And my mother. I've been so desperately trying to keep from being rejected that I have been keeping people away. I need people, but I don't trust them. I do stupid things, and feel stupid doing them, just to be liked. I have been paying ten years for what he did to me, and for my mother not believing in me. I've paid enough."

Nicole thought for a moment. "What are you going to do?"

"This is a start," said Kathy, pushing an envelope over to Nicole. "It contains all the things I've wanted to say to Frank all these years. I confront him with what he did and what it meant to me. I demand an apology. I tell him what I want from him. I'm going to write one to my mother next. Read it."

Nicole opened the letter. "Dear Frank," it began.

INSIGHTS

As we grow up, our world expands. We are learning machines, soaking up facts and impressions about the world like sharks in a feeding frenzy. We digest these by placing them into our internal world view. We work hard at integrating new learning with the things we have learned before. We struggle to understand things in a way in which our world and our lives make sense.

We need to have our world orderly, to have it make sense and not be chaotic. This allows us to trust it enough to risk ourselves in the process of growing and changing. If we can't trust the world, we can't change and grow. We can't risk loving others or investing in a challenging career. If we can't trust the world to be orderly, we cannot believe that our life efforts will pay off.

Some experiences are so frightening and overwhelming that they challenge our view of the world as being orderly. As a result of major accidents, abuse, or other kinds of victimization, we learn to experience the world as chaotic and capricious. We lose our trust in the world and do not believe it will support and nurture us. We can no longer approach the world with a basic optimism, an "existential faith," and trust that it is, on the whole, a safe place. We become so fearful of others that our attachments bring us pain, and we avoid them in the future. We may end up believing there is purpose in our striving. Our basis for self-esteem and self-respect is threatened.

Thus, as a result of being traumatized, we may learn the following rules of living:

▼ Don't believe

▼ Don't trust

▼ Don't care

▼ Don't invest

▼ Don't love yourself

Some traumas, such as Kathy's, happen over an extended period of time. In our efforts to survive the situation, we adopt coping strategies. We may:

▼ narrow our awareness to include only what is of importance to get through alive

▼ become vigilant and suspicious of every possible threat

- ▼ become emotionally detached

- ▼ become stubbornly determined just to "get through"

- ▼ suspend our belief in ourself, our judgments, our abilities

These emergency coping systems work for us, and we do get through. Because they work, and because of the tremendous stress caused by natural reactions to our world coming apart, we tend to maintain these coping systems. They become lifestyles.

Even long after the traumatic events are over, these reactions can become a way of life. Our further development may be hindered by our constricted, survival-based world view. Many of the problems we now face, such as substance abuse, codependent relationships, and compulsive disorders develop from attempts to cope with long-term reactions to earlier traumas.

In order to recover from the traumatic experience, we must overcome these coping systems. Healing requires us to regain our unity with the world by:

- ▼ rebuilding a more realistic way of looking at the world, one that allows options and growth

- ▼ reestablishing trust in the world that it will meet our needs

- ▼ reattaching to people, things, and conditions

- ▼ recapturing a sense of meaning, purpose, and direction

- ▼ learning to accept and love ourselves again

In order to overcome the self-limitations of our coping systems, we must open ourselves to the incident itself. We must relive the incident so that we can release the life energy that has been diverted to protect us from pain. We must release the incident and the pain so that we may recreate our unity with the world.

The healing process begins by our retelling the story of our hurt in its fullness. In order to protect ourselves from the pain, we created originally an incomplete, partial story of the incident, one we could tolerate. In order to let go of the fears, pain, and protective lifestyles, we must fill out and complete that story. The central process includes preparing ourselves for the talk, reliving

83

the incident, releasing the feelings, filling out a more complete version of the incident, and sharing the complete story with others.

Just as Kathy discovered, this can be a difficult task. It can call up painful and frightening memories. Sometimes these memories are overwhelming in intensity and cause distress, particularly if the coping strategies such as alcohol, drugs, and food are no longer available.

For this reason finding support is critical. Try to get several people to agree to be listeners. A listener is someone you can talk with about the exercises, your experiences, and your reactions to dealing with your past trauma. Ideally, a listener is someone you can trust with sensitive or potentially embarrassing information. Choose someone you are certain will not use the information against you or attempt to act in your behalf.

Additionally, it is important to know how to contact a mental health professional in case your reactions are more serious than you anticipated. Finally, dealing with past trauma can be stressful. Find ways to take good care of yourself while you work on your past hurts. Don't make big decisions, don't take on extra work, and don't act quickly without thinking through the effects of your actions. Get enough rest, eat well, exercise, and make sure you have time alone to think. Consider keeping a journal of your personal reactions and discoveries during this very important time.

Here are some things to watch out for when you deal with painful memories. If you experience:

▼ problems with thinking, flashbacks, disorientation, fears of "losing your mind," or difficulty coping with ordinary life tasks

▼ waves of uncontrollable emotions such as fear, sadness, despair, or hysteria

▼ unfocused agitation, ritualistic or uncontrolled behavior, inability to care for yourself, or thoughts about violence or ending your own life

you should see a mental health professional as soon as possible, for these could be symptoms of a larger problem.

There are many delayed stress responses to trauma. Substance abuse and other compulsive behaviors are among them.

Often attempts to break such habits are made more difficult because of leftover pain and confusion. Breaking through this pain is sometimes necessary to break through problem behavior.

You may have heard about a condition called Post-Traumatic Stress Disorder. PTSD is a disease caused by exposure to severely stressful events such as deaths, life threat, or victimization. PTSD victims exhibit many symptoms, but key signs include flashbacks, nightmares, fears, avoidances of people or places, emotional outbursts, and oversensitivity. Sometimes PTSD results in the same sorts of behaviors which may have brought you to this book: substance abuse, self-destructive behavior, compulsions, or other problems of living. One of the exercises later in this chapter will help you determine if you are exhibiting signs of PTSD for which professional assistance will be helpful.

But you don't have to have PTSD to suffer from past hurts. And whether you have it or not, your efforts toward recovery may go a lot easier if you are able to let go of those hurts, stop looking back, and start moving into your own future.

EXERCISES

The following specific signs may indicate that you are suffering from PTSD, or one of the other post-trauma effects. Check those which apply to you:

___ reexperiencing an event through flashbacks, preoccupation, or nightmares, having feelings that it is happening again, or distress in similar situations

___ having fears, avoiding similar situations, avoiding thought and feelings associated with an incident

___ feeling numb, not being able to feel feelings you think you should, losing interest in things which previously interested you, believing that you won't live long

___ being irritable, jumpy, or overreactive, having trouble concentrating or trouble sleeping

If you have checked any of these, you may be suffering needlessly. Consider seeing a qualified mental health professional—your recovery and your future happiness might be at stake.

The following exercises are designed to help you let go of prior hurt and begin the natural process of healing. It is advisable that you go through these exercises with a counselor or at least with a trusted, responsible friend with whom you can share your pain.

Be aware! If you find yourself being bothered by the exercises, becoming depressed, or starting to have nightmares or some of the other symptoms previously listed, don't procrastinate. Something is bothering you and you need to find out what it is. *Go in and check it out with a counselor!*

Telling Your Story

Everyone has a story. A story about a tragic event, and for better or worse, how it shaped life's circumstances. Most young people have experienced at least one very difficult experience, such as the divorce of their parents, the death of someone close, or a serious accident. Many have experienced several, or even a whole series of unfortunate events. These experiences can teach us negative things about ourselves or the world. They can lead us to the sort of negative activities, patterns, and habits we now are trying to turn around.

In order to complete these exercises, focus on one incident which was particularly difficult for you. Pick the worst if you can. If it seems overwhelming, then choose a less intense incident. You can repeat the process with other incidents when you are ready.

Telling your story involves several steps in order to get the most out of the process. In these exercises you will be challenged to enter into dialogue with yourself and deal with your own past in ways you may never have dreamed possible. Here you may begin to tell your own story about the hurts in your past. You should:

▼ *Properly prepare yourself*
   This task will not be easy, and it cannot be done by someone else. Whether through group involvement, prayer or meditation, service to others, or writing, you must find a method that works for you. You must prepare yourself for the work involved in your healing.

▼ *Relive the incident*

You must allow your memories in. As much of the memory "data" as possible must be recaptured and relived. You must reexperience the incident and your reactions as completely as possible.

▼ *Release the feelings*

You must become aware of your deep feelings about the incident, about others who were involved, and about yourself. You must begin expressing those feelings to yourself and to others. Only then will you be able to release those feelings and free yourself.

▼ *Complete the story*

Your partial, distorted version of the incident must be completed in full form. This completed story, if true to your experience, combines the intensity of the moment with the perspective of the ensuing years. It is an expression of a very important part of you. It is your story, and a part of who you really are.

▼ *Go public*

You must go public with your story. You must allow selected others to know what you have been through and its importance to you.

While you work on this chapter, keep an eye on yourself. Each of the stages of your crisis experience brought you a barrage of sensory experience, impressions, reactions, and interpretations. Our memory records each of these sensory inputs separately. What we experienced and what we recall are two different things, however. The main focus of the experience is all we can usually recall. Yet what was important at the time may be only a partial interpretation. We were struggling at the time to keep order and avoid harm. In emergencies, our mind tends to simplify and attend only to what is necessary for survival. Much important information gets ignored. Later, when we are safe, we try to reconstruct what happened. The main memory of events which our mind focused on at the time is the memory we will recall. But there is more data available which can give us different perspectives.

You will explore each stage of your crisis in this section. In some of the sections, you will answer general questions about your experience. In others, you will recall specific sensory memories. Some may be easy, some quite difficult for you. You will probably find all of them interesting.

*S*etting the Stage

What background factors set the stage for your crisis? What did you bring to the incident which allowed it to become critical for you?

Let's explore some of the possible elements. Several things could have set you up for your reaction to this incident. You may have been sensitized to this type of incident through early family conditioning or events. Earlier traumas or other learning experiences could have left you particularly vulnerable. You may have been experiencing pressures from home or work which combined to stress you out before the crisis even began. Or you might have had unrealistic expectations which caused you to evaluate your own performance and reactions too harshly.

Think about each of the following background factors carefully. Write down which factors you feel might have been compounding your situation. Use short phrases, sentences, or even brief paragraphs if possible. If the space in this book is not enough, or not private enough, get a lined notebook and write more complete responses in there.

Were there family themes or issues involved in this incident? Think about early family experiences and relationships. Did any family emergencies occur which resemble this experience? Can you recall incidents, anecdotes, or even family stories that are similar to the crisis? Did your family give messages to you about yourself or the world which might have affected how you responded to this crisis?

Did the type of incident have some particular meaning which was especially difficult for you? Did it challenge aspects of you which you don't feel good about, such as being flawed or inadequate? Were old wounds reopened? For instance, if this incident involved loss or victimization, had that ever happened before?

_____

_____

_____

_____

Did you go into the situation stressed out already? What was going on at home or at work which could have set you up for your reaction to the crisis? Had you been going through difficult personal changes which had you stretched out thin already?

_____

_____

_____

_____

Had you ever thought that this sort of thing could happen to you? If you did, did you imagine that you would be strong, calm, competent? Did you think that you would fall apart? What did you expect of yourself?

_____

_____

_____

_____

89

*R*ecalling the Event

Sights, sounds, odors, tastes, touches, body sensations, and feelings are the building blocks of memories. Each step of a crisis is experienced with those sensations, and each sensory memory combines with others to complete the memory of that step. To adequately tell the story of your traumatic experience, you must start by gathering the sensory data and combining it together.

If this event was traumatic for you, it was probably emotionally overwhelming, and full recall may be difficult for you to recall it fully now. Before you start it might be a good idea to take some precautions:

- ▼ Give yourself plenty of time. Once started, you will want to take as long as you need to get what you came for.

- ▼ Make sure you have privacy, so you can become absorbed without interruption.

- ▼ Have a support person available. This could be a family member, a trusted friend, or a professional.

- ▼ Consider debriefing with someone afterward, to share the memories, feelings, and things you have learned. Talking is an excellent way to sort things out.

- ▼ Exercise and burn off some of your body's chemical response to the powerfula memories.

- ▼ Plan a reward. Be good to yourself. Buy something nice. See someone special. Go somewhere that feels good. Whatever you consider a reward, do it—you've earned it!

Sights   As you recall the event, first focus only upon your visual memories. Start with the most obvious people, action, and events. Write them down in short phrases. Then relax and go through the incident again. Look for details. Can you see things you missed before? Write down details you remember, even if they don't seem important.

Look at the scene from different perspectives. Look for things you might have missed before. Check out colors, textures, actions, and faces for new meanings. Look for details in the outer edges of your picture. Imagine looking at yourself at the time, and notice how you looked. Float over the situation, looking at it from above.

_____

_____

_____

_____

Sounds Take the same approach with the sounds you remember. After you are relaxed, set up the situation visually and then include the sounds. Begin to focus more upon the sounds you hear. Separate different sounds from one another, looking for the significant ones. After you have isolated some sounds, become aware of how those sounds affected you. Listen to them over and over, and feel your deeper response. Pay attention to the impact each of the sounds had and has upon you. This includes background noise, conversations, and other sounds which you now understand to be important in the situation. When you write down the sounds, try to name the sound, describe it, and relate your response to it.

Now go back and write down each sound fragment you recall.

_____

_____

_____

_____

Odors and tastes Odors and tastes add a dimension of realism and sensory enhancement to good food, short stories, and memories of the past. Relax again. Recall the sights and sounds of the incident. Then open your memories to the scents and tastes of the moment. When you write them down, try to both name and describe each scent and sound, as well as place them in context. When you write them down, tie in each with the associated sights and sounds.

_____

_____

_____

_____

91

Touch During the incident you may have had some sort of physical contact. It may have been as subtle as the feel of your clothing or movements, or as commanding as pain. You may have been injured. You may have touched or been touched in ways that impacted you. Relive the event, focusing upon touch (skin sensation) or body sensations (deep tissue sensation, movement, or physical reaction). Relate memories of skin touch and bodily sensations such as pressure, temperature changes, or physical action.

Describe each in terms of what happened and how it felt.

_____

_____

_____

_____

Feelings It is often very difficult to remember the things we felt in a crisis situation. Usually we feel a lot, and often more than we can easily recall. Often we remember one predominant feeling, to the exclusion of several other, often conflicting, feelings. Our mind helps us survive the crisis by automatically going into tunnel vision, but the feelings and "unimportant" details are often still there.

It is helpful to have some reminders at this point. Here is a list of 120 frequently-experienced feelings. The emphasis is on negative emotions, those most likely to arise in a crisis.

Now read the sights and sounds sections again. Close your eyes, and recreate the situation in your mind. Look around and notice more details. Replay it, focusing more on your own reactions. Then go over the list and look for each feeling in your recreated scene.

alert	excited	alive	sensitive
strong	good	anticipating	amused
capable	happy	sure	untroubled
secure	determined	concerned	appreciated
respected	empathetic	elated	enthusiastic
daring	smart	courageous	suspicious
disgusted	resentful	bitter	fed-up
hateful	listless	moody	lethargic
gloomy	dismal	discontented	tired
dejected	unhappy	bored	bad
forlorn	disappointed	weary	frustrated

sad	depressed	sick	disconsolate
dissatisfied	fatigued	angry	hurt
miserable	pained	lonely	cynical
exhausted	indifferent	unsure	impatient
dependent	unimportant	regretful	torn-up
inadequate	ineffectual	helpless	resigned
apathetic	shamed	worn-out	useless
weak	hopeless	forlorn	rejected
guilty	worthless	impotent	futile
abandoned	estranged	degraded	puzzled
edgy	upset	reluctant	timid
mixed-up	baffled	nervous	tempted
tense	worried	troubled	frightened
anxious	dismayed	apprehensive	disturbed
shocked	panicky	trapped	horrified
afraid	scared	terrified	threatened
sullen	provoked	contemptuous	disdainful
alarmed	annoyed	antagonistic	vengeful
indignant	mad	confused	alienated

Now write down the feelings you marked, putting short phrases where possible (for example, instead of "anxious," it may be more complete to say "increasingly anxious" or "more and more anxious as time went on"). This may take several attempts, or even several writing sessions to complete. Modify and revise the list continually, as new memories emerge.

_____

_____

_____

_____

Your Reactions Some responses to critical incidents are quite normal. These are universal thoughts, feelings, reactions, and behavior that are signs of stress and reactions to emergencies. The following list may be helpful in recalling your response to the full-impact stage of your incident. Go through the list and circle those reactions you experienced at the time.

Thoughts	*Reactions*
confusion	sweating
time distortions	pale or flushed skin
impaired thinking	fainting
mental slowness	headaches
thoughts out of control	nausea/vomiting
problems prioritizing	staring, dull eyes
problems making decisions	

Feelings	*Behavior*
fear	irritability
anxiety, clinging to others	hyperactivity (too fast)
explosive anger	hypoactivity (too slow)
intolerable frustration	aimless wandering
unusual lack of reaction	lack of control
	detachment

If your experience feels complete, fine! Remain open to new memories, details, nuances, or perspectives that may come in trickles or bursts during the day or night.

If your experience feels incomplete, that's alright too. It is all part of the process. You may wish to return several times to repeat the exercise, and if you do, you will probably get more each time. Give yourself time.

If you have uncovered things you can't cope with, or if this approach simply is not working for you, then you may want to consider seeing a professional for help. Get someone who is experienced with trauma, and someone you can trust. Be gentle with yourself.

*A*ftershocks

After the crisis resolved, after the dust had settled, was it really over for you? For some, the end of the crisis is only the beginning of the pain. The full impact of the event is not felt until later. Sometimes days or weeks, sometimes months or years go by before the most troublesome reactions to crisis surface. And sometimes traumas leave scars which seem permanent.

In the next section we will explore some delayed reactions you may have had to the crisis you experienced. First we will look at external changes in your life caused by the event. Then we can think about some of the internal changes. Finally, we can assess whether those internal changes developed into lasting problems.

Changes Outside

Crises upset the things that form the structure of our lives, and that we depend upon for our sense of security and belonging. They are the things we count upon to make our achievements, our values, and the realization of our dreams possible. Crises often strike these structures directly, and our lives are altered.

Six facets are central to our lives' structures: our physical capabilities, our families, our close friendships and social relationships, our standards of living, our important geographical locations, and our future options.

In answering the following questions about external changes, take your time and think about each one carefully. Answer in full sentences, including as much detail as possible. Try to indicate what each change meant to you, how you felt about it then, and how you feel about it now.

How were your physical condition and capabilities changed by the incident?

_____

_____

_____

_____

Was your family changed? How?

_____

_____

_____

_____

How were your social relationships and close friends affected?

_____

_____

_____

How was your standard of living and physical security changed?

_____

_____

_____

Were special places and locations which had important meaning to you altered or destroyed?

_____

_____

_____

Were your future options affected by the crisis?

_____

_____

_____

How has your present situation been shaped by that incident?

_____

_____

_____

Changes Inside

Changes outside of ourselves hurt us and bring about changes within. We may lose our bearings and our sense of direction. Our lives may be derailed for a while in ways we did not expect. We struggle inside to adapt to the changes outside.

Just as our reactions to the crises themselves were complex, our later reactions can be diverse and confusing. They can also be much more intense than we expect. Sometimes people worry that they are losing their minds because of delayed reactions to incidents. These reactions affect our thought patterns, our feelings, our physical condition, and our behavior.

It might be helpful to look at some common delayed reactions to crisis:

Thoughts	*Reactions*
trouble planning	fatigue
preoccupation with incident	increased illness
orientation toward past	physical concerns
fear of "going crazy"	psychosomatic illness
denial of incident, or its importance	weight change

Feeling	*Behavior*
depression	problem sleeping/nightmares
grief/loss	social withdrawal
fear of reoccurrence	compulsive talking about
anxieties/panic	incident
inappropriate anger	avoidances
unusual fears	family problems
oversensitivity	drinking or drugs
inappropriate crying	rapid lifestyle changes
	problems at school
	sexual acting out
	running away
	problems with the police
	flashbacks

In looking over these reactions, you may have recognized some of your own. In developing a full account of your experience, you will need to include your delayed reactions.

Write a sentence or so describing each of your own later experiences. It might be helpful to mention about how long after the incident each occurred.

Delayed thought reactions

trouble planning

preoccupation with incident

_____

orientation toward past

_____

denial of incident or its importance

_____

fear of "going crazy"

_____

Delayed emotional reactions
depression

_____

grief/loss

_____

guilt

_____

fear of reoccurrence

_____

anxieties/panic

_____

inappropriate anger

_____

unusual fears

_____

oversensitivity

_____

inappropriate crying

Delayed physical reactions

fatigue

increased illness

physical concerns

psychosomatic illness

weight change

Delayed behavioral reactions

problems sleeping/nightmares

social withdrawal

compulsive talking about incident

avoidances

drinking or drugs

family problems

_____

rapid lifestyle changes

_____

problems at school

_____

sexual acting out

_____

flashbacks

_____

problems with the police

_____

It is quite likely many of the changes you have written about went away over time. It is also likely some of them didn't, and those that didn't are the roots of what led you to this book.

Which of these changes are still going on? Have they settled into a repetitive cycle that still bothers you? Go back over this list and circle those inner changes that are now a problem for you.

You might also have been affected in less obvious ways. Because of past hurts, many people are so fearful of further hurt they never take chances, never learn to live. They may adopt a lifestyle of avoiding relationships, success, and potentially rewarding adventures to protect themselves from any possible chance of further trauma.

In what ways have you limited yourself because of the incident?

_____

_____

_____

_____

Other people are affected the opposite way. They seem to be

drawn to risky situations or situations resembling the incident during which they were traumatized. Sometimes this is almost like an addiction. Other times it is an attempt to reconstruct the traumatic event so that it can be mastered. In what ways have you made life choices, adopted styles, or pursued interests because of the incident?

_____

_____

_____

_____

_____

*U*nfinished Business

Sometimes traumas leave unfinished business. Kathy needed to say several things to her stepfather. Until she does, she will be unable to leave the trauma in her past. While we may never be able to undo the damage or rewrite history, we may be able to change the way we feel about the incident and about ourselves by taking action. Kathy's action was to write her stepfather and mother separate letters.

Unfinished business may be taken care of by:

▼ writing letters

▼ confronting people

▼ taking particular actions or participating in symbolic rituals

▼ visiting the trauma site

▼ communicating with others who were there

▼ receiving apologies or amends

▼ speaking out publicly or taking political action

In general, the world can hurt us more than we can ever hurt back. But taking action on our own behalf is healing. Even if we can't change things, we must try in order to regain our self-respect and dignity.

Do you think that you might have things that you have to do before you can put the incident to rest?

_____

_____

_____

_____

_____

Congratulations! You did it! Or, rather, you are doing it. You'll probably discover as time goes on that you will find yourself thinking about this more and more. New memories may arise and new connections will be made between what happened long ago and what happens in your life right now. That's good! That's healing. Be open to these revelations and make all the additions and changes to your lists that you want.

Share your work on this chapter with your listener now, if you haven't already. As you remember more and make more sense of your experiences, share your work with others.

6

Accepting Losses

Many people carry a special burden through life. It is an unseen weight upon their souls that they are trying to forget. Sometimes they use compulsions, problem behaviors, substances, or other addictive agents to self-medicate their pain. Frequently, they have no idea they are carrying this load. The burden they carry is the pain of loss.

This chapter is for you if you have undergone loss in your life. It helps you work toward accepting that loss and understanding the way in which the loss helped lead you to your problem behavior. If you have not experienced loss in your life, then you may skip this chapter and move ahead.

Before you do, however, you might just look it over. You may surprise yourself with the losses you really have experienced and the pain that is still alive.

SYLVIA

It had come up almost without warning. Sylvia had been sitting in English class listening to the teacher discuss a poem by Dylan Thomas. She suddenly found herself plunged into a deep sense of sadness, deeper than any she had felt before. The poem had been about death, and how one should fight dying. It was stirring for Sylvia, and a little frightening.

When the bell rang she gathered her books and left with the others. She had PE next, but couldn't bring herself to dress into her gym clothes. She retreated to her old sanctuary, the library. Finding her accustomed seat in the back, she laid her head on the desk. She desperately wanted to eat. Determined to resist the urge, however, Sylvia put away her thoughts of cookies and chocolate.

"What's this all about?" she wondered. The poem seemed to trigger it, or maybe it was something the teacher said. The poem was about fighting death. But I'm not sick, and no one I know is dying. Maybe it's about other kinds of losses. But what? The waves of sadness hit again, and she cried softly. Instead of fighting the crying, she let herself feel it. It was as if the sadness was an old acquaintance, or someone who had been around for a long time. It was familiar, even though she didn't understand it.

Walking home, Sylvia was preoccupied with the lingering depression. She came to the same wall she had sat on months ago after she had first been caught in the bathroom. She sat again on the same spot. It seemed comforting somehow. Curiously, she began to notice that when she fought against the sadness, she felt anxious, but when she gave herself over to the sadness, she felt different. Sometimes she would get angry, sometimes more deeply depressed, and sometimes even strangely comfortable. She felt for a moment like a research psychologist with a white coat and clipboard, running experiments on her own feelings.

One thing particularly puzzled Sylvia. It wasn't so much the image of dying that brought on the sadness, but rather her fighting it. This was confusing. Of course you should fight death! Living is worth keeping, and dying is frightening. As the poet had said, it is a mark of human dignity to fight to live. Why would fighting death be a problem to her?

▼ ▼ ▼

The overcast sky let little light through the curtains of Dr. Perez's office. It was warm inside, and the muted colors seemed as comforting as the hot tea Sylvia was sipping. Dr. Perez listened closely while Sylvia related the sudden, overwhelming feelings of sadness she had been experiencing. She took several notes and seemed thoughtful.

"So who died?" she asked abruptly.

"Excuse me?"

"It sounds as if you have suffered a loss," Dr. Perez suggested.

Sylvia thought. No one recently. Her whole life seemed to be a process of washing up on a beach and dying. Who died? "Nobody in particular," she replied.

Dr. Perez was quiet.

"Unless," added Sylvia almost as an afterthought, "you consider my sister."

Dr. Perez' eyebrows raised.

"My sister died when I was seven. She was fourteen and got sick. I was too young to remember anything."

"Many people remember a great deal that happened when they were seven years old. Especially if it was something important," said Dr. Perez.

"It wasn't much. We don't talk about it a lot."

"What do you remember?" probed Dr. Perez.

Sylvia thought. She told Dr. Perez about visiting the hospital. She recalled her parents calling her into their bedroom early one morning, telling her that her sister had "passed on." Sylvia remembered asking when she would be back. Her mother had left the room, and her father hadn't said much. Later that day her parents had gotten all dressed up and left her with a baby-sitter. Then they had come back and people had brought over food, and other people came and stood around talking quietly. Her sister's room had remained unchanged for several months until Sylvia had been moved into it.

"Did she have a name?" asked Dr. Perez.

"Angela." said Sylvia. It felt strange to say her name aloud.

Dr. Perez looked at Sylvia with one of those "now-think-carefully" looks. "Were you the bearer of Angela's life?"

"What?"

"Sometimes family members refuse to deal with their grief. Sometimes they will keep the deceased's room intact as a shrine, refuse to get rid of his or her clothes, never mention the deceased's name, or pressure another family member to take over the deceased's role."

"Yeah?"

"Yes, the things the deceased was expected to do. You said earlier that Angela was the smart one, the one who was to go to college and succeed, while you were the baby. Everyone let you get away with murder. You were allowed to do pretty much what you pleased. That changed with your sister's death, didn't it?"

Sylvia remembered her first report card after Angela's death. Grades had never mattered before. Her father had frowned and said that things were going to have to change. They got her a tutor. Her room had to be tidy all the time. Nobody seemed interested in who she was anymore, only whether she did well. "I think so. Suddenly I was expected to be perfect."

"Your family may have been attempting to keep Angela alive through you. They simply transferred all the dreams and goals they had for her onto you, as if by you accomplishing them, Angela would still be alive. Did they speak of Angela very much?"

"It was something we never mentioned." Sylvia was quiet for some time. It was still strange to hear her name aloud.

"There's another problem in all this, Sylvia." Dr. Perez spoke slowly and with compassion. "Because you have buried your grief all this time, you haven't been able to express or even acknowledge your anger at having to live your sister's life instead of your own. To get angry would be to admit you have something to be angry about—your loss. In order to protect yourself from the pain of grief, you have been blocking your anger at how unfair everything is."

Sylvia sipped her tea and thought.

▼ ▼ ▼

It was now evening. Sylvia spread old family pictures and mementos out across her bedspread. There were some of Angela, a few of herself, some together. She realized there were quite a few more of Angela than of herself. Another interesting thing, she noted. Almost no pictures were taken after Angela's death.

There were also a number of newspaper clippings, report cards, awards, and other documents. Most of these were Angela's. Those of her own were more recent, following Angela's death. It was almost as if she, Sylvia, hadn't existed until Angela died.

Sylvia thought about this. She remembered what Dr. Perez had said about her having to live Angela's life. She hadn't believed it, or more accurately, hadn't really understood it at the time. Yet here, spread out before her, was evidence. Her parents had saved all of Angela's things, and only after Angela was no longer available had they started to save pictures and papers about Sylvia.

And Sylvia hadn't really noticed. Sylvia reflected on how the pressures on her to get good grades, get on the honor roll, join the right clubs had increased yearly. She had been pushed to join team sports and take part in school plays. At just fifteen years old she was expected to choose the right college and declare a major. And never, never complain.

106

Sylvia got a piece of paper and started a letter to her sister. She knew that Angela couldn't read it, but it seemed important to get some things off her chest. She wanted to let Angela know how she felt about her dying. At least let her know the little that she understood. And she wanted to let her know that at last she had some idea of the pressure under which Angela had lived. "Dear Angela," the letter began. "I've never written to you before, but here goes . . . . "

▼ ▼ ▼

Several nights later, the family sat down to dinner. Conversation was limited to the normal surface small talk. Sylvia was midway through her meatloaf and mashed potatoes when a question popped into her mind and wouldn't go away. Her father paused for a moment in the middle of another long account of the latest political atrocities in Washington, when Sylvia cut in. "Was Angela in pain when she died?"

No one spoke or moved for a full minute. At last her father broke the silence. "No. She was unconscious. Pass the meat, please." Her parents awkwardly resumed eating.

"I mean," Sylvia persisted, "what did she die of?"

"We'll talk about it later," said her mother. Sylvia knew that they wouldn't.

"Mom," Sylvia tried one last time, "I really have some questions."

"No!" shouted her father. "You're disturbing your mother!"

This time Sylvia didn't try again. She left the table and went back to her room. It's true, she thought. Dr. Perez is right. They really don't want to believe that Angela is dead. But she is. Sylvia sat on her bed, looking at a picture of Angela she had stuck in the frame of her dressing table mirror. Angela really is dead.

Her weeping began gently with a welling up of tears. But soon she was crying in earnest. Burying her head in her pillow so her parents wouldn't hear, Sylvia wept in great, deep, heaving sobs. Years of loss, years of repressed feeling poured out into the pillow.

▼ ▼ ▼

Bare trees reached toward a gray sky. It was quiet, almost serene in the cemetery. Sylvia sat by her sister's grave in the cold afternoon, deep in thought. It was almost as if her sister could hear.

"Well, Angela," thought Sylvia. "You were always the accomplished one. You did everything right. Everything, that is, except die.

But you know what? Angela, I never knew you." The tears ran down Sylvia's cheeks. "I never even knew who you were when you were here. I was only seven when you died. I can never know what you would have been like now. Or forty years from now. We could have known one another. You could have known the person I have become."

Despite her tears, or perhaps because of them, Sylvia could feel the anger and resentment beginning to melt. First she had to play the supporting role of "little sister." Then she was cast as Angela herself. Feelings frozen for many years began to thaw. And in place of the resentment the deep sadness she had felt before returned.

"I'm now a year older than you were when you died," she thought. "If you were still alive, you would be twenty-two. Would you be out of college already? Or have a job? Would you be married? Have kids? I would be an aunt. If I was an aunt, I would be the very best, like Aunt Julie. I would be there for your kids when they needed me, Angela."

Aunt Julie. Aunt Julie had always been there for Sylvia. She had answered questions which no one else would answer. Julie would have known Angela well because she lived so close to them. She would be able to tell Sylvia more about Angela. Sylvia smiled.

▼ ▼ ▼

Aunt Julie's kitchen was so cheerful. They lunched on sandwiches and cocoa. Julie had invited Sylvia over immediately and seemed to welcome Sylvia's questions. "I'm glad you're starting to ask about these things," Julie reassured Sylvia. "It's been so hard watching you suffer, and not being able to help. I just had to be patient and wait until you were ready. I figured you would come when it was time."

"Aunt Julie, I didn't even know there was anything to ask about. I have so many questions, about my family, about why Angela died, and about myself. But can we start with Angela? Who was she? What was she really like?"

INSIGHTS

As we grow, we inevitably lose things. Important people may die or move away. We may leave a beloved place, or that place may change. We may hold comforting beliefs or have values which we outgrow. Parents divorce, pets die, friends grow up and go away. Treasured objects are stolen. Even our successes bring about change. We cannot live and grow without experiencing loss.

When we lose someone important to us, we go through a process of detachment so that we are free to reattach and love someone else. While we cannot replace dear ones, we must be able to reinvest ourselves in new relationships or else we go on forever holding onto the past. By holding on to the past and fearing the future, we live constricted lives. We must let go in order to move on. This process of detachment is not easy.

The first reaction to sudden loss is usually shock. All but the most expected and routine losses take us by surprise. We are stunned and often quite disoriented. Our worlds are shaken. Things feel unreal. While we may have very strong initial emotional reactions, very quickly we become numb and unfeeling. We may become detached from things, or even unable to function.

After the shock wears off we pull ourselves together and go through the motions of coping and getting our lives back together. We go back and forth between being functional and falling apart. We may be greatly fatigued and yet have difficulty sleeping. We may feel anxiety, anger, or even guilt. In order to manage the intensity of our feelings, we may deny the severity or even the reality of the loss itself. We may minimize its importance, or distort it in our thinking. Our upset may show in our thoughts, feelings, reactions, and behavior as we struggle to comprehend and accept the loss. Like Sylvia, we may stop at this point in our grieving process, living in a way which allows us to put the grieving on hold indefinitely.

Sylvia did not remember her first reactions of shock, nor her later feelings of sadness until she worked with Dr. Perez. She had shut down on her feelings of loss because they were too painful, and because her family demanded it. She learned that she had to let go of her loss or remain chained to the past, uncertain of the future, and dysfunctional in the present.

To move forward in our grieving involves suffering. We experience loneliness, helplessness, and exhaustion, as well as fears about an uncertain world. We begin to question whether our reasons to go on are worth the pain we must endure. Now that Sylvia has opened herself to this suffering, she can complete her grieving.

In order to reach a full acceptance of loss, we must put the relationship into proper perspective. The meaning of the relationship must be understood and honored, and then it must be given over to the past. Emotionally, we must clean house. We must express whatever emotions have resulted from the loss, including owning up to both the good and the bad. We must complete unfinished business, including saying things that were unsaid, doing things left undone, and letting go of the rest. This often results in deep sorrow and even depression.

Once Sylvia moves forward with her grieving, she can begin to rebuild her life. She can turn around her eating problem because she no longer needs the emotional cushion it provides her. She is free to be open to her deeper feelings and her life.

If you are having difficulties with yourself or your relationships, or with your school and work, you may be suffering from an earlier loss. Unresolved loss can underlie acting out, attitude and mood problems, compulsive behavior or addictions, and underperformance.

You can suspect unresolved loss if you:

▼ have periods of sadness and crying for no reason

▼ drink, use drugs, or do other forms of self-medication

▼ have not grown according to your own expectations

▼ avoid dealing with painful issues

▼ avoid good-byes

▼ are unable to leave relationships that are not good for you

▼ do not make life changes that are potentially good

110

▼ do not help others to change and develop themselves

▼ have trouble taking reasonable risks

▼ unduly fear rejection or abandonment

Our problem behavior may be hard to change if we have suffered loss and our grieving is unfinished. We may be either trying to ease our pain or avoiding commitments in our lives by engaging in our problem behavior.

However, our ability to turn our life around depends upon facing up to our prior loss. This takes courage and perseverance. Time must be spent developing awareness of the loss and remembering the events surrounding it. Feelings—past and current—must be expressed. Telling the story of the loss and its meaning is as important in dealing with loss as it is with prior trauma.

Grieving past losses does not need to be as painful or lengthy as we might think. We are used to the pain already; it has fashioned our lives and our problems. Understanding helps a great deal, as does revisiting important places. Relaxation and imagery can be very useful in making the memories more bearable. Sharing the pain with others is helpful as well.

Finally, there is another, different way in which loss affects us. If we are trying to let go of problem behavior, we must appreciate that it, too, is a loss. Our "problems" were once solutions. They gave us comfort, relief, excitement. If they hadn't, we wouldn't have allowed them to become a part of us. Now we are trying to cut them out of our lives. If Sylvia wants to give up abusing food, she must face up to the loss involved. Otherwise, she will not understand why she sabotages her own recovery. It hurts to lose things which are important to us, and we resist hurt. As strange as it sounds, grieving the loss of our problems is part of the solution.

EXERCISES

Losses we do not recognize, or ones that we have minimized or ignored, can pose a major roadblock to recovery. They can stand in the way of letting go of our problems. These exercises are designed to help you explore losses you have suffered in the past or are suffering in the present. They will help you let go of the past and let go of the things that are holding you back now.

The exercises are meant to be done in order, and are likely to cause you to do a lot of thinking about your past. To benefit the most from them, it would be helpful if you kept a journal. Find a notebook that feels right, and make a paragraph or page entry every day. This will not only pull things together, it will be interesting for you later. Write about your reactions to the exercises, memories that come up, conversations you have, feelings you experience, and even dreams you have during this time.

Another good idea is to pick someone who would be a good listener and talk to her or him every now and then about your work in this chapter. If you worked through the last chapter on trauma, you probably already have people picked out.

The following exercises are written as if the loss was a person, such as a parent, brother or sister, or friend. If the loss you experienced was a place, time, object, or relationship, reword the question appropriately.

*S*igns of Unresolved Loss

Rather than starting with the losses themselves, let's begin by seeing whether you experience signs of losses that are still bothering you. If you experience any of the following symptoms, you may suffer from unresolved loss. Circle any that apply to you:

unhappiness

irritability

depression

difficulty with relationships

school and work problems

compulsions or dependencies

acting out

attitude and mood problems

underperformance

lack of personal growth

avoidance of painful issues

avoidance of good-byes

inability to make life changes

inability to take reasonable risks

inability to help others to change and develop

periods of unexplained sadness or crying

avoidance or fear of new "loves"

You may also experience the following symptoms related to the experience of the death itself. Again, circle those that apply:

flashbacks

avoidance of certain locations, situations, themes

specific fears, anxieties, preoccupations

nightmares

attempts to relive, master the incident

If you have experienced some of these, the death may have been traumatic for you. You may benefit from going back and working through the previous chapter, *Letting Go of Past Hurt.*

*I*dentifying losses

While some people get to adolescence without any significant losses in their lives, most have some. Some have many. Here is a chance to identify the different losses in your life—or situations that may have made you feel like you lost something.

death of a parent	divorce/separation
death of a relative	stepparent/stepsiblings
death of a friend	loss of physical capabilities
death of a teacher	death of a pet
serious illness/ hospitalization	moving out of a community or area you loved
boarding school	having a friend move away
foster home	a change of school
theft/home destruction	having a new sibling who your
loss of a love relationship	parents favor

Which of these, or others, have you experienced as being serious?

Loss: *Your age:*

_____   _____

_____   _____

_____   _____

_____   _____

_____   _____

On the following time line, mark approximately when each loss occurred:

|_____|_____|_____|_____|_____|

birth   2   4   6   8   10   12   present age: _____

For each loss you have listed above:

How close were you? _____

How much did he/she mean to you? _____

What were the circumstances surrounding the loss?

_____

How have you coped since the loss?

_____

Which one or two of the losses listed above do you feel was the worst for you? Why?

_____

_____

In the exercises that follow, focus upon the loss that you remember to be the worst. After you complete the chapter you will probably wish to go back and repeat the exercises for each of the losses you have listed as being serious for you.

Before moving on, however, think for a moment about the worst loss. Consider what that person meant to you prior to his or her death.

Write three significant incidents you recall involving that person:

1. _____

_____

2. _____

_____

3. _____

_____

How much did she or he mean to you?

_____

_____

Do you have any other special memories of that person, particularly memories involving the rest of your family?

_____

_____

_____

*L*iving through the Dying

Your experience at the time of the death of someone close to you can leave a lasting impression. It helps to recall just what happened to free up those memories and give them the perspective your current age provides. Think about where you were when you first became aware of the death, and the events that occurred during the following days.

What do you remember about the actual death? What events took place, and what do you remember doing?

_____

_____

_____

_____

_____

Can you remember how you felt when the person died, or after you heard about the death? Use the following words as reminders.

alert	excited	alive	sensitive
strong	good	anticipating	amused
capable	happy	sure	untroubled
secure	determined	concerned	appreciated
respected	empathetic	elated	enthusiastic
daring	smart	courageous	suspicious
disgusted	resentful	bitter	fed-up

hateful	spiteful	listless	moody
lethargic	gloomy	dismal	discontented
tired	dejected	unhappy	bored
bad	forlorn	disappointed	weary
frustrated	sad	depressed	sick
disconsolate	dissatisfied	fatigued	angry
hurt	miserable	pained	lonely
cynical	exhausted	indifferent	unsure
impatient	dependent	unimportant	regretful
torn-up	inadequate	ineffectual	helpless
resigned	apathetic	shamed	worn-out
useless	weak	hopeless	forlorn
rejected	guilty	worthless	impotent
futile	abandoned	estranged	degraded
puzzled	edgy	upset	reluctant
timid	mixed-up	baffled	nervous
tempted	tense	worried	troubled
frightened	anxious	dismayed	apprehensive
disturbed	shocked	panicky	trapped
horrified	afraid	scared	terrified
threatened	sullen	provoked	disdainful
contemptuous	alarmed	annoyed	antagonistic
vengeful	indignant	mad	numb

Write down the feelings you experienced, using short phrases where possible (for example, instead of "anxious," it may be more complete to say "increasingly anxious" or "more and more anxious as time went on").

_____

_____

116

_____

_____

_____

_____

_____

_____

Did you attend the funeral or memorial service? Do you remember anything about it? Write down any particular memories (sights, sounds, impressions, reflections) you have of the service:

_____

_____

_____

_____

_____

Can you recall how you felt at the time? Use the above list of feelings as reminders. List them:

_____

_____

_____

_____

_____

A eulogy is a reflection upon a person's life. It includes basic biographical information such as the person's birthdate, birthplace, family, career, and major events of his or her life. It also tries to comment upon the significance and meaning of the life. Find the eulogy from the funeral if available. Add words to it from your own memories. If one is not available, write one yourself.

Here's a major project: Make a scrapbook about the person for posterity. This could serve as a living memory of the person's life and will provide relatives and descendants with an idea of just what he or she was like. You could include the eulogy you have written, letters, clippings, photographs, testimonials from others, or any other mementos you want.

117

*W*hat It Has Meant

In this section we explore the implications of the loss. The information gathered here will give clues to what the loss has meant to your life during the years since the death.

On the following time line, mark the major events which have occurred in your life since the person's death:

|_____|_____|_____|_____|_____|

At the person's death   now

Your age at the time: _____   your current age: _____

Had the South won the Civil War, had the Japanese not bombed Pearl Harbor, had John F. Kennedy not been president, things might have been very different for the United States. The same is true for you. Things might have been very different for you, had your loss not occurred. Sit back for a moment and speculate. How might things have been different?

Might things have been easier or harder? Might you have developed differently? Might you have made different choices in your life?

_____

_____

_____

If this person was really important to you, then you had part of your life tied up in her or him. You may have identified with her or him, or perhaps you were in some way dependent. If nothing else, the death may have meant some change in your way of life. Looking at it from this perspective, what part of your life was lost when she or he died?

_____

_____

_____

How about the rest of your family? How has the loss affected them as individuals and how has it affected your life together?

_____

_____

_____

Sometimes a loss is very painful. So painful, in fact, that we can't talk about it even with those who are close to us. And when we can't do that, it can drive a wedge between us. Who haven't you talked about the loss with (either in your family or outside of it)? Is this something you need to do?

_____

_____

_____

*G*rieving

You may have a lot of sadness and pain locked inside of you. You will not be able to move on with your life unless you release those feelings. Grieving is the process of expressing the feelings that loss has created.

If you get stuck in this section and find it too hard to do, or if you find yourself overwhelmed by the feelings that come up during the exercises, do yourself a favor and get some assistance. Find a counselor whose job it is to help people express, heal from, and learn from their reactions. Life is too short to waste because of embarrassment, false pride, or fear!

Here are some things you can do to help let the feelings out:

▼ Visit important places that you and the person who you lost shared

▼ In your journal, keep a record of these visits. Fill out the following questions while you are there:

Date: _____ Place: _____

I remember coming here with: _____

When: _____

I remember the following things happening:

_____

_____

_____

_____

Being here now, I am feeling:

_____

_____

_____

I need:

_____

_____

_____

▼ Do something you liked to do together. Fill out the same form as above.

▼ Visit the grave if possible. Imagine that he or she can talk to you. Begin by sharing all of the things you have written so far. Let your conversation ramble, and catch him or her up on your life. Leave feelings of embarrassment and self-consciousness at home, because this is much more important to you than anything others might think.

▼ Write a letter from the person who died to the rest of the world. In it, imagine that you are that person, writing to explain why you lived the life you did. It could be titled, "In my defense."

▼ Spend some time interviewing people who knew the person. Find out how they saw him or her, interesting anecdotes they can recall, and what he or she meant to them.

▼ Write the deceased a letter. Express what she or he meant to you. Express how you felt about the death and how you feel now. Bring up any unfinished business, say any things which were left unsaid. Say good-bye to her or him.

▼ Hold a ritual reburial. Put copies of the letter or other mementos in a box and bury it, burn it, or take it somewhere and leave it. Dress appropriately for the occasion, and have a speech and prayers prepared. Consider inviting others, particularly family members along. Spend time giving vent to feelings.

- ▼ Set aside time alone to cry, express anger, or whatever else comes up. Light candles, play appropriate music. Let your feelings loose.

- ▼ Share your experiences doing these exercises and your grief with your listener and others close to you.

*R*ebuilding

Ever since this person died, you have been building your future. If the unresolved loss kept you from growing in important ways, the future you have been creating has been artificially limited in some ways. Once you have been released from the bondage of the past, you are free to fashion a fuller future.

One reason we resist letting go of important people is that they provide direction and support for us. If they were important, it was because they met some of our needs. Once we let go of those we have lost, those needs must still be met and we must find new ways to meet them.

With fewer limitations, your life may prove to be quite different from what you previously expected. What would you like to see happen, if more was possible? On the following time line, make some speculations about your future. Indicate what you would like to achieve, accomplish, experience, or create:

|_____|_____|_____|_____|_____|_____|

your present age _____ the age you want to live until _____

How are you feeling about this future? Refer to the list of feelings on pages 115-116, and write down those which apply:

_____

_____

_____

_____

_____

What personal traits, values, and resources did you gain from the person who was lost that you can use in meeting the future you wish to fashion?

Traits:

_____

_____

_____

_____

Values:

_____

_____

_____

_____

Resources:

_____

_____

_____

_____

Think about the various people around you (family, friends, teachers, or community members) who could assist you in creating that future.

Family members who will support my efforts:

_____

_____

_____

_____

Friends who will support my efforts:

_____

_____

_____

_____

Community members or resources who will support my efforts:

_____

_____

_____

_____

Sometimes our first attempts at resolving our past losses prove to be only partially successful. One indication is if the symptoms of grief which you identified earlier in these exercises persist. It may be that there are other losses you still need to deal with, or that you need to do more work. Try repeating the exercises with greater openness to the feelings. If you are still unable to move forward you should consider seeing a counselor or attending a grief group in your community. Also, family pressures may be working against your efforts. If that is so, the next chapter, *Taking Care of Family Business,* may be helpful.

7

Taking Care of Family Business

In the fifties, the Palo Alto Veterans Administration Hospital had an excellent new treatment program for seriously disturbed patients. It was a success, and eventually the program directors realized that their patients needed some sort of reward for their unexpected progress. What could be better, they thought, than weekend passes home? After some thought and planning, they began issuing passes to those patients who were the most recovered.

Later, while evaluating the effectiveness of the program, they made a startling discovery. In most cases, patients who had been given weekend visits home had returned worse than when they left! After much thought and debate the program directors were forced to conclude that home was not a good place for their patients.

How could this be? After all, home is where the heart is. Home is our source of nurture, our sanctuary from life, the place that we always wish to return to. Or is it? For many, the reality may be very different. For many, the family is not only the original source of the problem, but the major obstacle standing between them and getting well.

Families are normally a problem for adolescents. The whole point of adolescence is becoming independent and establishing an identity apart from the family. Yet there are equally normal pressures to remain in the family. Your parents will resist your attempts at independence because it means a change, because they worry about your choices, and because they know the dangers of the adult world. And a part of you fights against the pressures and isolation that adult responsibilities bring.

Addictive or compulsive behavior makes the transition harder still. Further, if your family itself has problems, your task is doubly difficult.

Recovery is not easy. The support of your family members—or at least their not pressuring you to remain dysfunctional—would be very helpful. Yet you may have already discovered that the family remain more of a problem than a solution. Understanding why and how they work against your recovery can help you decide how to manage them so you can make the turnaround you deserve.

JASON

"Come in and sit down!" Mike's cheerful voice called out. Jason closed the office door behind him and took his usual seat across from Mike's desk. Mike smiled a welcome but quickly came to the point. "Jason, your parents aren't coming. They phoned and said they would see you at home. I'll give you a ride after our meeting."

Jason wasn't surprised. It wasn't the first time they let him down, and he knew it wouldn't be the last. It was a little sad, though. He had graduated from the program, and this was his exit interview. Parents were supposed to be there. "Oh well, . . . " he said.

"We pretty much thought this might happen," reminded Mike. "They only made it to a couple of family nights." He leaned back easily with his hands behind his head, looking at Jason. "You know, your recovery over the next few months is not going to be easy."

"Why do you say that?"

"Jason, you've come a long, long way in this program. Remember when you wouldn't admit you had a problem? You even ran away. Through your own efforts and through your faith, you've been able to turn things around."

Jason smiled. It felt good to hear it. He had come to trust Mike's compliments and not look for some kind of ulterior motive. "Thanks. You guys are the best."

"Remember when we talked about our parents?" Mike asked. "We said that the single most important thing they could provide was consistency."

"Yeah, I do," acknowledged Jason, "and my parents were not consistent. They painted a great picture—looking good to others—but when my father drank and when they would fight, I got ignored. Sometimes I had to take care of myself for days. And the worst part was that they would go on as if nothing had happened. Everyone was supposed to play happy."

"Jason, your drinking was, is, your attempt to gain control over how you felt. By controlling the external reality, alcohol, you attempted to control your inner reality, your feelings and experience. To a certain extent it worked. Now, staying sober depends upon finding better ways to control your reality."

Mike continued. "Your family hasn't changed. Tonight's no-show proves that. You are going to have to learn how to handle your reactions to their inconsistency in order to stay sober. It's going to be tough, because you not only have to fight your urge to drink, but also your family."

"I know," admitted Jason. "It's been that way for a long time."

They were quiet for a while, each into his own thoughts. Their conversations were like those between old friends. Mike spoke first. "Remember that time we talked about family resistance to change?" Jason nodded.

"We said that some families actually work at keeping their members dysfunctioning." Mike shifted in his chair, leaning toward Jason. "This is going to be like a game. A very serious game. Your recovery will depend upon whether you can figure out why they need you to have a problem, and how they work to keep you drinking."

▼ ▼ ▼

They were finishing dinner. Jason's mother was starting to clear off the table. "Jason, we're going to church tomorrow morning. Please try to be ready to go on time. We'll leave at 8:45. I ironed a white shirt for you."

"Uh-oh," thought Jason. "Here it comes." He gathered his strength and said, "Umm, Mom, I'm going to be going to our old church down on Stanford Street. I've already talked to Father Jenkins about it."

Mom stopped. "What? But . . . that's quite impossible. Your father and I have been looking forward to us all being together again at our new church tomorrow. Our friends are expecting to see us."

"I know how you feel, Mom," Jason began, "it's just that . . . "

"No!" His mother interrupted. "No." She threw an I-expect-you-to-bail-me-out glance at her husband.

Jason's father pushed the last of his dessert around with his fork, unable to avoid involvement any longer. "You know, Jason, we're proud of the way you finished your program. It's time to get back to normal and be a family again." He got up and began pouring himself a drink out of the decanter which sat on the buffet table. "We want you to join us tomorrow."

"But Dad," protested Jason. "I don't know anyone at that church. I feel comfortable at our own church."

"Well, we don't," his mother said sharply. "Dear. . . , " she looked again at her husband.

Jason's father was clearly getting irritated. He put his drink down on the table firmly. "I don't want to hear any more about it. We leave at 8:45 for our church."

Jason looked at the drink, then at the decanter, and back at his parents. He stood up, went to the front hall closet, got his jacket, and left the house.

He walked toward town. He was steamed, and he wasn't sure where he was going. One thing was sure, however. He had to get away from that house.

Lost in his thoughts, he didn't hear the car approach behind him, slowing alongside. "Yo, Jason!" a voice called. Jason looked over to see his old friend Aaron. He recognized Sammy's car.

"So," he called back, "it's the two Musketeers. How're you guys doing?"

"The *three* Musketeers, now." corrected Aaron. "Jump in." With nothing better to do for the moment, Jason jumped in.

"So how was the funny farm?" asked Aaron as they drove on. "Did you let the head mixers get to you?" He broke open a beer. "There's more back there," he nodded toward the back seat of the old sedan.

"No, thanks, Aaron. It wasn't bad."

"Do they still have the point system? They did when I was there. Hey, we heard you broke out and totalled a car. That was bad!"

"Yeah, they've still got it." replied Jason, feeling uncomfortable. "Where're you guys headed?"

"The usual, lookin' for a party. Know where one is?"

"Nope." Jason thought about it. He was tempted, and the beer smelled good. On the other hand, this was beginning to look like a real

127

typical scene, driving nowhere, looking for a party. He was quiet while the others talked. Then he came to a decision. "Look," he said finally, "would you do me a favor? Drop me over at the church?"

"What?" asked Aaron. "Why there?"

"I want to see if they have a meeting tonight."

"Yeah, sure," replied Aaron, obviously disappointed. "Whatever . . . . "

▼ ▼ ▼

"Hi. My name's Bruce, and I'm an alcoholic and addict. This is the regular meeting of Overcomers Anonymous."

"Hi, Bruce," came the reply from the fifteen or so members sitting around the circle.

Bruce continued. "For those of you who are new, Overcomers Anonymous is a nonprofit organization whose purpose . . . . " Jason was surprised at how similar this meeting was to those at Haven House. After Aaron and Sammy had dropped him off, he only had to follow the signs to find the meeting. He was nervous about attending, but at the same time he was relieved there was a meeting to go to. He wasn't sure what else he would have done. In fact, he still wasn't.

"Tonight we're going to talk about 'Enabling'," said Bruce. "I know that I personally have struggled with an enabler all my married life, and that I have struggled with being an enabler myself. Has anyone else ever lived with someone who helped him or her continue doing what they shouldn't do?"

As several people spoke about enablers in their lives, Jason thought about his. His parents made it so easy for him. They gave him all the reason in the world to drink. Drinking had been a way to strike back at them. They couldn't stop him, and drinking had provided him a relief from the pressure. Openly leaving alcohol around wasn't the problem. They conveniently looked the other way, covered up for him, excused his behavior, and constantly bailed him out to protect their own image. That was the problem. He had appreciated the enabling and certainly used it to allow himself to get away with drinking. Now it was dawning upon him just how damaging their enabling had been.

"Has anyone else had a difficult time because of enablers?" Bruce asked the group. No one spoke. The silence was uncomfortable, but Jason fought against the impulse to break it. What could he possibly offer? He didn't really even know what he would say.

"I have," Jason heard himself say. "My parents always told me not to drink, but never drew the line unless it inconvenienced them. I just got out of a sixty-day program and I'm sober. But it's hard. Tonight they started in on me again." Jason's voice broke, but he controlled it and kept on. "I'm scared that I won't be able to handle it. I'm afraid I'll blow it."

"Jason," Bruce spoke softly, "it makes us sad to find out that our parents can't be what we need them to be. But sometimes that's just the way it is. One of the things that I have found helpful is a way of looking at it. I ask myself the question: "Does this person need me to drink?" Or sometimes I ask, "What does my drinking buy them?" When others are invested in my having a problem, I have to find a way to protect myself. What can you do to protect yourself from your parents?"

▼ ▼ ▼

It was quiet in Mike's office. Jason had come to enjoy his after-care meetings with Mike. "Tell me, Jason, how have things been going this week? You mentioned that you've been attending the Overcomers meetings as well as ours. Helpful?"

"It is. I get different things from each."

"What's the most useful part of your program right now?"

"Probably the 'Parenting Yourself' lectures."

"What have you learned?"

"Well," Jason sat back, "I've learned that my family has a lot of problems they can't solve yet. I knew that, but I always figured the biggest problem was me." He grinned. "It isn't me."

"It must feel good to find that out," commented Mike.

"It does. I have been a problem, but I'm finally beginning to understand I have been *a* problem, not *the* problem. My family is pretty messed up."

Mike thought for a moment. "You said you thought your family needed you to drink. What do you mean?"

Jason became quiet. "You know, my parents have always fought. They even split up three or four times. But they always wanted other people to think nothing was wrong. It could never be their fault. They need to have a reason that caused it. I was the reason. As long as I was drunk, they could blame me and not have to deal with each other."

"It sounds like you've been moving fast," reflected Mike. "What have you learned about taking care of yourself at home?"

129

"I learned that I can only take care of myself. My parents have to row their own boat. I've got to keep out of the way when they're having problems."

"How about your problems?" asked Mike.

"I can't expect them to help me with my problems. They just don't have what I need. I've got to take care of business myself."

"And what if the problem is bigger than you are?"

"Well," Jason answered, "then I just have to get help."

▼ ▼ ▼

It was late in the evening when Jason got home. He found his father in the study, drink in hand. He didn't look drunk, just sort of detached. "Hi, Dad. What's up?"

Dad looked at him. "Where have you been?"

"At a meeting." To his surprise, Jason's father seemed to accept this. Jason asked "Where's Mom?"

"She's gone to bed. She's tired." He didn't say anything while Jason sat down. Then he spoke again. "We had a fight." This admission surprised Jason, but he remained quiet. "I don't know," his father continued. "It doesn't even matter what it was about. We seem to fight just to fight." He waited for Jason to say something. With Jason's assistance not forthcoming, he went on. "I've been thinking. Maybe we should see a counselor. What do you think?" He looked at Jason.

Jason stood to go up to his room. "I hope you can work it out, Dad. Good night."

INSIGHTS

130

Not everyone who has a problem comes from a problem family. But a great many of them do! Understanding your family is important for three reasons.

- ▼ Your family experiences may have a lot to do with why you *started* your problem behavior.

- ▼ Your family may have a lot to do with why you *keep* your problem.

- ▼ Your family may actually work against you in *getting rid* of your problem.

Families are pretty complicated. In order to get a better understanding of how to deal with them, it helps to have some basic concepts. First, it has to be understood that families are systems. This means that they consist of interconnected parts, and that the functioning of each part will affect each other part. This is important, because you may have begun your problem behavior because of the effect the rest of the family had upon you. Further, certain family members may have done things in a way that made it easier to keep your problem alive. Finally, the family may, for reasons we will discuss, actually make it very difficult for you to quit, despite anything else they say. Because your family is a system, you must plan how to manage it in order to overcome your own problem.

When you think about it, it doesn't make sense that your family members would try to keep you dysfunctional, especially if they spend a lot of time and money trying to help you change. But look at it this way: the daily activities in a household are complex. Food must be provided, clothing readied to wear, cleaning done, repairs made, emotional needs have to be met, and dignity maintained. All these activities, from the most lofty to the most basic, are important and must be coordinated. If each of these tasks had to be approached as if for the first time, with all decisions needing to be made anew, and all of the techniques and procedures worked out from scratch, the activity of an average family in a single morning from 6:30 A.M. to 8:00 A.M. would be staggering, and things would grind to a halt. The family, just like any organization, must be able to count on routine.

Routine involves shared expectations. Like the members of a pit crew for a race car, each family member needs to be able to count on a certain predictability. Our roles within the family define what we can expect from others, and what others can expect from us. Each role, once worked out, has a place in maintaining the complex order of family life. Consequently, each family member is encouraged—even pressured—to fulfill his or her role. Even in families where an individual is cast in a "sick" role (like the "problem child" or the "drinker") the other family members have spent a great deal of time and energy working out their own roles to accommodate that person. They tend to accept and even encourage the behavior. This allows them to go on with their lives without having to stop and rethink all of their own plans and routines.

While healthy families encourage gradual growth and change within members, this may not be so with unhealthy families. Their need for stability becomes a stranglehold on individual change, and any demands for adjustment are felt to be overwhelming. Even change for the better may be resisted. Family traditions become stagnant, communication is restricted, and stony silence and rigidity replace support. While the members of such a family would never admit to themselves that they did not support your recovery, their day-to-day behavior can create tremendous obstacles for you.

Further, your problem behavior may be important to your family members. They may use it to avoid their own change. Parents who are undergoing conflict between themselves may prefer to confront your problem instead of their own. Families in which one parent is alcoholic or suffers from other problem behaviors may welcome a diversion, and treat your problem as if it were *the* family problem. Your problem may be used by the family as the cause of *their* problems, even if it is not.

Here are some general strategies that can help in dealing with your family if they seem to be working against your recovery:

▼ Awareness is the best defense. Whenever you run into family difficulties that make your recovery hard, ask yourself, "In what way could this be protecting them from having to make their own changes?"

▼ Consider the possibility that their resistance to your change might be the result of misunderstanding. Ask yourself, "Have I made my intentions clear?" Also ask yourself, "Do they know why I'm doing what I'm doing?"

▼ Examine the way you are approaching them. Could you be too forceful, too unbending? Ask yourself, "Have I given them a chance to be heard?" Also, "Have I really let them know that I have heard them?" Think about whether you are being unnecessarily inflammatory. Ask, "Am I using language that distracts from the real issues?"

▼ Consider the effects of your actions upon each of the other family members.

▼ Anticipate their fears. Reassure them about what you are *not* going to do which they may be fearing.

▼ Don't try to challenge them about their own shortcomings. Lead by example.

If you really want to change some things about yourself, you have to start by figuring out your family's role in your problem. You need to get a better picture of your family members, how they operate, and what they do to you. You need to understand your parents' style of parenting and how that affected you in the past. You need to understand the overall emotional climate of your family and how that pushed you into adopting a coping style. You need to know what that coping style is and how it slows you down now. And finally, you need some alternatives. You need to work out a plan for dealing with your family in a better way.

No one issues how-to instructions with babies. Raising them is definitely a "learn as you go" business. Bookstores are full of parenting how-to books but only a small percentage of parents buy and read them. While you have to get a license to be a doctor, drive a car, and even cut hair, you do not need a license to be a parent! As a result, there are many bad parents around. The overall style of parenting with which you grew up may have fallen short of giving you what you needed. Reflecting on your parents' style of parenting may give you information about how you can parent yourself better now and give yourself the guidance and support you need.

Troubled families create stress; children growing up in troubled families must cope with that stress. If that is your background, it is likely that the strategies you learned to handle the stress have contributed to the problems you are now facing. Recalling your coping style and linking it to your current problems may give you insight into the steps you need to take for the future.

What was the general climate of your home? Some families are supportive, challenging, loving, or strong. Others are not. Troubled families raise children who reflect that trouble. While some children are more resilient than others to the influence of the family, it is nevertheless useful to get a picture of your family's climate in order to further understand the origins of your problem behavior.

*E*XERCISES

The following exercises are designed to assist you in coming to grips with your family. They will help you get a better picture of your family, how it operates as a unit, and what it does to you. Your parents' style of parenting, and how that affected you, the overall emotional climate of your family, and how that pushed you into adopting a coping style, and how your coping style slows you down now will be addressed. Finally, you will be able to work out a plan for dealing with your family in a better way.

*P*arents

Parents build families and shape children. If they do a good job, the children tend to thrive and grow strong. In fact, it is amazing just how many parenting mistakes children can take without developing lasting problems. There are limits, however, and children can suffer harm through consistently poor parenting.

Some types of parenting are particularly hard on kids. If you grew up with parents who were so distracted with their own problems that they didn't have the time or energy to give you what you needed, you may still be needy. If they were unable to provide consistency or leadership, you may still be seeking those things. If you grew up unloved, you may spend all your time searching for love.

All of us need to believe in our parents, especially if we have reason to doubt them. So we tend to be overforgiving and deny their faults. This means that we blame ourselves for our shortcomings. But look at it this way. It is one thing to accept responsibility for what you need to change; that's good. It is quite another, however, to deny how you got that way. That keeps you from changing it. You need to understand the origins of your problem in order to deal with it.

Often, personal shortcomings can be traced to the way your parents treated you. In fact, some specific personal profiles are associated with particular parent styles.

Do any of these profiles fit you?	*If so, your parents may have been:*
anxious (insecure, negative, hostile, lacking self-esteem, jealous)	rejecting
submissive (dependent upon others, lacking self-esteem, slow, lacking self-reliance)	overprotecting, dominating
impulsive (selfish, demanding, rebellious, lacking responsibility, unable to tolerate frustration)	overpermissive, overindulgent
rigid (guilt-ridden, lacking spontaneity conflicted, overly conscientious, self-condemning, needing to please, procrastinating)	perfectionistic, demanding
lost (confused, lacking self-identity or initiative, having a poor self-image, looking for stable values)	inconsistent, inadequate
angry (having problems with friends, hating parents, aggressive, fighting authority, self-destructive)	over-punishing

If any of these profiles fit you, your parents may have related to you in the manner listed. Circle the profile or profiles that fit you. Describe how the profile fits your family experience.

Ways your parents fit the profiles:

_____

_____

_____

Ways in which they do not:

_____

_____

_____

Reasons you might have to let them off the hook, or be extra charitable in your judgment:

_____

_____

_____

What did you miss getting from your parents that you needed?

_____

_____

_____

How could you get that for yourself now?

_____

_____

_____

*F*amily climate

Parenting styles contribute to the general climate of the home. The word "climate" refers to the overall atmosphere and character, such as whether the family is strong, nurturing, and supportive or is weak and unstable. The family climate describes the environment within which a child is brought up, and can influence whether a child will grow to meet his or her potential, or may grow anxious, fearful, and troubled.

The four general family climates that lead to later problems for children are weak, hostile, disturbed, or broken. Here is a self-assessment questionnaire to help you see if your family fits one of the four problem profiles. On the lists below, check the ones that apply to you and your family:

W*eak*** The weak family is unable to provide strong leadership, guidance, resources, and support to its children. This may be due to the parents' lack of ability, resources, or both.

___ Does your family have difficulty coping with the ordinary problems of living?

___ Does your family lack resources, require outside assistance?

___ Do your parents have certain inadequacies (mental, maturational, educational) resulting in incompetence?

___ Does your family have trouble adjusting to changes?

___ Are your parents unable to provide their children with security and guidance?

___ Are they unable to assist in the development of basic competencies and self-esteem?

H*ostile*** The hostile family lives by and for conflict. As a result, children are subjected to a climate of fear where they are denied the opportunity to develop their talents in a supportive, nurturing environment.

___ Is there a great deal of fighting, nagging, belittling, or annoying behavior in your family?

___ Do family members experience much frustration and dissatisfaction?

___ Is there poor communication in your family, leading to arguments and fighting?

___ Is there a lack of consistency in the enforcement of rules?

___ Are children unable to learn to communicate, trust, or establish solid relationships?

C*razy/Addicted*** The crazy or addicted family is erratic, inconsistent, and in turmoil. Usually one or both parents is disturbed, dependent, or both, but sometimes it is just the interaction itself that is crazy. Children growing up in such a home are deprived of stability and predictability and have little chance of security.

___ Are one or both parents emotionally disturbed?

___ Are one or both parents dependent upon some sort of substance or compulsive behavior?

___ Is there a great deal of emotional turmoil, which is easily started and never solves anything?

___ Are children deprived of the stability and love they need?

___ Are children pulled into the emotional conflicts between parents?

___ Does the disharmony result in a threat to family security?

*B*roken   The broken family often lacks the sense of secure continuity that a two-parent family can provide. Whether the break-up occurred because of death or by choice, children can be left without the support they are used to.

___ Is the family split apart because of death, divorce, or separation of parents?

___ Do the children often feel conflicting loyalties, and pressure to prefer one parent over the other?

___ Do the children live in fear of rejection and abandonment?

___ Are the children deprived of stability or love?

___ Are one or both parents so caught up in their own grief or need to recapture their own youth that they are emotionally unavailable to their children?

If you had a large number of "yes" answers to one or more of the sections above, it is highly likely that your family fits that profile. It is also highly likely that you had to do considerable adjusting and adapting to grow up in that family.

In families such as these, often at least one of the parents is alcoholic, violent, depressed, or has some other disability that renders him or her unable to parent. A word often used to describe this person is "dysfunctional," which means he or she cannot function the way a person should.

A family with one dysfunctional parent might still be able to handle the situation. Often, however, the other parent is not able to cope well and may fall apart. Sometimes he or she is unable to force the dysfunctional parent to get help. Whatever the reason, a parent who allows the other parent to continue dysfunctioning is called an "enabler" or a "codependent." The enabler lets the dysfunction go on and adds to the children's stress.

From the child's point of view, family rules are sometimes nonexistent, sometimes overenforced. Sometimes the parents are present and supportive, sometimes not. Sometimes home is a safe place to be, sometimes it is dangerous.

The question now is, if your family was like this, what did you do to take care of yourself? How healthy was your coping style?

*Y*our Style of Coping

When your family is stressful to you, when the family climate is weak, hostile, crazy, or broken, how can you protect yourself? If your family fits one of these styles, you probably worked out a system of coping with the stress.

When secure and consistent family conditions are not available, children take defensive action and find ways to make the best of it for themselves.

Four basic styles of coping are common among children of weak, hostile, crazy or broken families. These styles are adapted from the work of therapist Sharon Wegsheider-Cruse.

*S*uperachiever   When the family cannot consistently meet the needs of the children, one child often takes over some of the parental jobs. This is often the oldest child, or second child if she is a girl. The superachiever sometimes cooks, does laundry, supervises homework, and puts the other children to bed. Often the superachiever holds a job and uses the money to buy food when the parents haven't done so. The superachiever grows up too quickly.

This role carries two major problems. First, as a mini-parent, the superachiever is deprived of a normal childhood. Second, because the parents have all of those obligations met for them, they stay stuck. The superachiever is an enabler to the dysfunctional parents.

In considering if you became the family's superachiever, answer these questions:

___ Did you spend more time taking care of others than of yourself?

___ When your parents were unable, did you cook, wash, and do the other household tasks they should have done?

___ Did you feel responsible for a parent's problems?

___ Did others in your family want you to take care of their problems?

___ Do you feel you should be a high achiever?

___ Do you tend to take things too seriously?

___ Do you feel that you must constantly earn the love of others?

Problem Child　When children's needs continually go unmet and they are deprived of affection and security, they get angry. Sometimes they act out that anger by getting in trouble. They may get rebellious and defy authority, or become aggressive or destructive. Other times they turn their anger inward, becoming depressed or even self-destructive. Delinquency, school problems, substance abuse, and emotional difficulties may all serve to send messages and gain attention. These behaviors are all typical of the problem child. Ask yourself the following questions:

___ Was you the one in the family labeled as the "problem child?"

___ Did you spend lots of time at the doctor's, counselor's or principal's office?

___ Did you have problems with teachers and school work?

___ Did you have run-in's with the police?

___ Did you get into early substance abuse?

___ Did you, or do you, have problems with relationships with others?

___ Do you have emotional problems?

Low-profile Child　When the family is unstable and things become uncomfortable, crazy, or even violent, one good way of

140

dealing is to keep out of harm's way. The low-profile child has taken this approach as a whole lifestyle. This person doesn't say much, blends into the woodwork, and hides when conflicts arise. In deciding if you became a low-profile child, answer the following questions:

__ Did you, or do you, avoid conflicts whenever possible?

__ Did you spend a lot of time by yourself?

__ Did you, or do you, avoid leadership positions?

__ Do you hold back?

__ Do you avoid confronting others, even when it's important?

__ Are you more afraid of being left out than being hurt?

__ Do you feel guilty or vulnerable if you stand up for myself?

Clown or Baby   Another role is the family baby or clown. This is often the youngest sibling or one who is treated as "special." This child is not held to the same expectations as the others and is cushioned from problems. The baby survives by being cute, or funny, often playing the part of the clown. Does this sound like you? Answer these questions:

__ Were you the "special one?"

__ Were you able to get away with things your other siblings were unable to get away with?

__ Were you able to turn away hostility or conflict by being funny?

__ Did you gain support by being "cute" or charming?

__ In school, are you the class clown?

__ Do you still try to charm people and get your way by winning them over?

__ Is it important, or safest, for you to be the center of attention?

In conclusion: does one of these coping styles fit you? Which one fits you best?

Sometimes we may alternate between one coping style and another. Sometimes we may develop from being one to being another as we grow older. Often our problem behavior—which we now want to change—started as part of our coping style.

Have you changed from one to another, or did you alternate between one or another?

_____

Which?

_____

Did your problem behavior arise as part of your coping style?

_____

How?

_____

_____

_____

_____

One of the major difficulties of taking on a particular role is that our family expects it of us and pressures us not to change. When we are trying to turn around behavior patterns that we no longer accept in ourselves, our families often are the ones to sabotage our efforts.

*H*ow to Swim Upstream

Change is hard. To try and change your own habit patterns is tough, and it takes a lot of energy. You need all the support that you can get from those around you. If you are willing to try turning yourself around, you would think that your family would be on your side and give you lots of support, right?

Not necessarily, as you have probably already found out. Over the years family members have gotten used to you. They have managed to work out their own ways of dealing with your behavior. Even though your changes would make things better for everyone, they are likely to resist. A well-known therapist named Virginia Satir had a good image to illustrate the interconnectedness of a family:

Imagine you are standing around with the rest of your family. All of you are tied to each other by lengths of string. You have a piece running from you to your Mother, another to your Father, and one to each brother and sister. They in turn are each connected to each other. Together, you are all part of a delicate, giant web that connects each of you. Now one of you decides to stand up on a chair and turn around. Everyone is pulled up by the change you have made and has to move in order not to break the strings that connect them. Some threads will inevitably be broken. New threads must be fashioned. Changes in any one person affect each of the others. It doesn't take long for people to get tired of being yanked around.

Whether your changes are for the better or for worse, they will affect the lives of other family members, who will probably try to cushion the blow. This means that making difficult changes in your life will be all the harder.

When changing results in family resistance, it feels a little like swimming upstream. The current is against you and sometimes it slows you down or forces you back. Like salmon leaping over small waterfalls, you may have to try some tricks to get around the resistance.

Here are some suggestions for dealing with family members who are holding you back:

▼ Look beyond the behavior to see the need. When people hold you back it is usually because they have a personal investment in things staying the same. They may need security, attention, or something else, and your change threatens their needs.

143

To help you sort through this, recall and write three ways particular family members can work to keep you from changing.

_____

_____

_____

What might be the real need that motivates them to do that?

_____

_____

_____

▼ Reassure the real need.

Looking at the real need, what could you say or do to help satisfy that need without compromising your need to change?

_____

_____

_____

▼ Hang tough. Change takes time and overcoming resistance takes a lot of time. In order for you to get what you want, you cannot give up until you get past the attempts to hold you back.

What can you do to help yourself hang in there?

_____

_____

_____

▼ Get some support outside the system. You need someone to acknowledge your efforts, celebrate your successes, and sustain you through the struggle. When your family can't give you that support, you need to get it somewhere else.

What could you do now to elicit support?

_____

_____

_____

From whom?

_____

_____

_____

When and how?

_____

_____

_____

*C*hanging Styles

What is the best way of coping with tough family situations? It depends. A good strategy in one situation might be terrible in another. Being assertive in a hostile situation may set you up for an assault. Keeping a low profile when you are being ignored or abandoned may keep you from getting what you need. Here are four powerful coping styles, but remember—they are only powerful in the right place!

*A*ssertive   Being assertive means standing up for your own rights. It means not being passive and not letting yourself be pushed around. But it also means not being aggressive. The difference between aggression and assertion has to do with personal rights. Aggression is when you stand up for your rights and ignore the rights of others. Assertion is when you stand up for your rights without depriving others of theirs. To be assertive means to speak out in defense of yourself.

Here are five ways to be assertive:

1. Avoid aggressive or passive behavior.

2. In any situation, ask yourself, "What do I want here?" or "What would be best for me?" Make your needs known.

3. Use the "broken record" technique: if someone is giving you all sorts of reasons why you shouldn't get what you need, keep repeating, "That may be the case, but I want _____." Don't be distracted, don't get out of control.

4. Make long-range plans for getting what you want. Write down all that needs to be done, first things first.

5. When you need others to do things for you, or to treat you differently, make a formal request for change: sit down with them; tell them what exactly they are doing

now that affects you badly; tell them exactly how it affects you when they do it; describe exactly what you would like them to do differently; request that they do it. (For example: "Would you please do such and such?")

Consider ways this suggestion might help in your situation:

_____

_____

_____

Self-contained Being self-contained has to do with no longer being an enabler. If you take responsibility for others and allow them to act in ways bad for them or for you, you help them to stay stuck. Being self-contained means taking responsibility for your actions and letting others be responsible for their own. When the other family members rely on you to take care of them, they are not doing either you or themselves a favor. To be self-contained is to look out for yourself and not take care of others when they can take care of themselves.

Here are five ways to be self-contained:

1. Take care of your own needs first.

2. Be clear about responsibility; know the limits of your responsibility.

3. Avoid enabling behaviors; ask yourself, "Will my doing this help this person to stay _____ (helpless, drunk, abusive, out of control)?"

4. Carry out your own obligations.

146

5. Find people outside your family who will help you get what you need and can coach you in dealing with family members.

Ways these suggestions might help in your situation:

_____

_____

_____

Low-profile Some situations are dangerous, physically or emotionally. When dealing with crazy, violent, or drunk people, it sometimes makes more sense to stay out of their way. Why get hurt if it will not change anything? To keep a low profile means to avoid standing out and attracting pointless abuse. This is a particularly powerful strategy in those situations where the problems occur in cycles. Be assertive when the violence or conflict is not a problem, but keep a low profile when it becomes mindless and intense.

Here are five ways to keep a low profile:

1. Become aware of cycles of hostility or craziness; when such conflicts occur, leave.

2. Avoid high traffic areas and areas of conflict.

3. Only enter into those discussions which are positive or have a strong likelihood of being productive.

4. Find out how to get help from the outside, if needed.

5. Look for indirect ways to get your needs met.

Ways these suggestions might help in your situation:

_____

_____

_____

Detached If our needs are simply not getting met at home, we need to take better care of ourselves. This means becoming less dependent on home for our emotional (and sometimes physical) support. We need to distance ourselves and become more detached. This is a more extreme version of being self-contained and requires reaching outside the family for assistance.

Here are five ways to become more detached:

1. Develop goals and attachments apart from the family.

2. Create a strong support system outside the family.

3. Learn to get your rewards from those outside of the family.

4. Avoid being pulled into family conflicts or flaps.

5. Find "chosen family" and spend time with them.

Ways these suggestions might work in your situation:

_____

_____

_____

Again, these four different approaches are powerful, but only in the right settings. And, they are suggestions only; each individual and situation is unique so there is no formula that works always. Everyone must work out his or her own best way.

The chart below offers a place for you to begin. First, find your *present* coping style on the left side. The adaptive goal shown next to it is where you want to get to. The next four columns show the strategy you should use to get there. Find your family climate at the top. Match the style with the climate, and you have your general direction. For example, if you are the problem child in a hostile family you probably should work at developing a low-profile style. This would help you handle the situation the best possible way.

Finding Your Adaptive Strategy for Family Change

Your Present Coping Style	Your Adaptive Goal	*If your family climate is . . .*			
		Weak	Hostile	Crazy/ addicted	Broken
		. . . your strategy is to try and be			
super-achiever	learning to let go	self-contained	low profile	detached	assertive
problem child	learning to be OK	self-contained	low profile	low profile	assertive
low-profile	learning to speak out	assertive	self-contained	detached	assertive
baby/ clown	learning to get serious	assertive	self-contained	self-contained	assertive

Here is an example of how the chart works:

If your present personal coping style is: <u>problem child</u>

and your family climate is: <u>hostile</u>

then the coping style the chart recommends is:

<u>to try and keep a low profile</u>

Now do this for yourself:

What is your present personal coping style?

_____

What was your family climate?

_____

What more powerful coping style did the chart recommend?

_____

Let's think a little bit about how you might use this direction.
Start by describing a difficult family situation that you have to
cope with frequently. Describe how it generally goes.

_____

_____

_____

_____

What do you now do to cope with this situation?

_____

_____

_____

_____

Now look at the power style the chart recommends for you.
Reread the description of the style and the ways to start. Think
about how those strategies might work for you in your situation.

Consider specific ways you could do each of those things. What else could you do to further your power style?

Write down a full list of all these strategies:

_____

_____

_____

_____

_____

_____

Consider this list a plan of attack. Use it. Copy it on a card and carry it around in your pocket until you need it, then pull it out to remind yourself of what to do.

Treat this like any other plan, and watch to see which parts work the best. You may soon find yourself handling those family interactions better than you had ever dreamed possible!

Outline other situations in which this strategy might work.

_____

_____

_____

Growing up is never really easy. Adolescence marks the transition from childhood to adult life, dependence to independence. At best it is frightening and challenging, at worst a nightmare. Whether good or bad, the familiar relationship between parent and child is stretched and ultimately transformed. Recovery issues cloud this already complicated picture. Learn, experiment, and become strong at dealing with your family. Do not expect overnight miracles. Be patient, keep trying new strategies, and stay with your struggle towards independence from the habits and dependencies of the past.

8

Settling Accounts: Steps Eight and Nine

Whatever caused your problem in the first place, whatever has kept it alive, and whatever pain it has brought you, one thing is certain. During the course of your suffering, your behavior has hurt others. And you know it. Despite what others may have done to you, you are responsible for whatever pain you have brought others.

It probably hurts to read that. It may even make you mad. But don't stop! It is important that you consider this thought. Your recovery depends upon it, and here's why:

Whenever we bring pain to others, we put ourselves off balance. Our actions cut two ways: we cause pain to those we have hurt and, in so doing, we lose some of our integrity. We experience guilt and shame for our wrongdoing. Guilt, shame, remorse, and imbalance are painful to us. If we are to gain inner peace of mind—the very thing we need in order to recover from our problem behavior—we must right the wrongs we have committed.

Step Eight begins this process by urging us to acknowledge our past errors:

8. Make a list of all persons you have harmed, and become willing to make amends to all of them.

Acknowledging the ways we have hurt others is necessary for healing ourselves, but it is not enough. We must act on our awareness and make appropriate amends.

Step Nine challenges us to act. We must follow our inventories by making direct apologies and restitutions for our past behavior:

9. Make direct amends to these people wherever possible, except when it would hurt them or others.

Our hurtful actions of the past can haunt us today. When we hurt others we cause anger and resentment. This serves to poison our relationships. Not only are others unlikely to help us when we need it, but the relationship itself will be unable to grow. We all need relationships to survive. If we do not maintain the ones we have, or if we do not learn to cultivate new ones, we will not receive the support and nurture we need.

This chapter explores how to go about righting past wrongs, how to straighten out your relationships and put them back on a sane footing. As Sylvia, Jason, and Kathy find, this task is very personal. Because of the different people they have wronged, the different types of wrong, and the uniqueness of each situation, each of them must discover his or her own way of making amends.

SYLVIA

Dr. Perez frowned. "Sylvia, I'm not sure I understand. You say you gave your parents a present and they didn't like it? So they didn't like it. What's the problem?"

"More than that. It was their anniversary and I gave them a picture of myself. They cried. Both of them."

"They were touched?"

"I guess . . . . But it was like they were genuinely sad."

▼   ▼   ▼

Sylvia is confused. Since working on the loss of her sister, things have been unbalanced between her parents and her. Sylvia has let go of much of her anger toward her parents, and has gotten to the point of even forgiving them for not seeing her as an individual. She is coming to understand that they have their own very real limitations. She is healing, but they are not. She is moving forward with her recovery and is ready to take on the next step—rebuilding her relationships. But her parents just are not ready yet.

▼　▼　▼

"Maybe they're still hanging on to Angela," Sylvia tried. "But couldn't they hold onto her without shutting me out?"

"Maybe it's something else," suggested Dr. Perez.

"Like what?"

"Like maybe they're mad at you."

"Because I lived and Angela died?" asked Sylvia.

"Perhaps. But it might be simpler than that. Maybe they're just plain mad at you."

▼　▼　▼

"Come on, Sylvia!" urged Louise. "Of course you know why they're mad."

They were walking under the canopy of camphor trees that lined the street near the school. The recent rain made the leaves slippery and the air sweet. "How many times have you told me about how you've shut people out and held back? You don't think that you did that to them?"

"But Louise," Sylvia protested. "Of course I did. Look at the way they treated me. 'Angela this,' and 'Angela that'! And all the expectations. They never once said 'Great job, Sylvia!' It was always 'Just a little harder, Sylvia,' or 'Have you tried such and such yet?'"

They waited for a light to change. "You know, Sylvia," said Louise, "I'm not saying that they did anything right. But look at it from their side. Nobody's perfect. First they lose one child. Then they don't do such a good job, and they lose the other. How do you expect them to feel?"

The light changed, and they crossed.

▼　▼　▼

She sat in the library, thinking about Raphael. They had gone together last year for nearly three months. The combined pressures of dealing with her parents, high school classes, and Raphael had just been too much. That was when Sylvia had started withdrawing and eating to excess.

153

It wasn't as if he had been hard to get along with. He was charming, friendly, and didn't pressure her for anything. But she had put up barrier after barrier. She would create arguments, not talk to him when he would call, and not meet him after promising to do so. She now knew why. Getting close to people was frightening; it put other people in the position where they could hurt you. So she kept him off balance. He had been confused and angry. Predictably, the relationship broke up after a while.

At the time she had told herself that she was too young for a steady boyfriend. That was probably true, but wasn't the real problem. The truth was that she had hurt him because of her own fears.

She still wasn't ready for a relationship with a boyfriend. Her dilemma now was how to let him know that it wasn't his fault things hadn't worked out, without leading him to believe that she wanted him back.

Sylvia gathered up her purse and books. She knew Raphael; apologizing to him face to face would just make things worse. But there was another way. She would write him a letter.

▼ ▼ ▼

She called them into the living room. Her parents were surprised at her forcefulness, but went along with it. They sat on the couch and she sat on a chair she had moved into just the right position. She had even made tea to serve them. It made her feel more in control of the situation.

"What's this about, Sylvia?" asked her father. He was not used to her taking the lead.

"Thanks for sitting down with me." Sylvia had rehearsed this several times, but it still felt awkward. "I have some things I need to tell you. I've ... "

"Sylvia," asked her mother, with a knowing look in her eye, "are you in trouble?"

Sylvia laughed. "No, I'm not. Well, I guess I have been in trouble for a year or so." Her parents looked more confused than ever. "You see, I have an eating problem."

Confusion changed to shock. "What do you mean ... " began her father.

"I'm a bulimic." She went on to explain what that meant.

"Sylvia, we didn't know!" her mother exclaimed.

"No, you didn't know because I kept it from you. It's really pretty easy to hide. In fact that's the main reason I need to talk to you. During the past year I've been hiding a lot from you."

Her father's eyes narrowed with suspicion. "This is because of Angela, isn't it?"

"No," Sylvia said. "This is because of me. By withdrawing from you, I've driven a wedge between us. I'm terribly sorry. I kept you from knowing your daughter."

*J*ASON

Jason and his father sat at the counter at Hoagy's Diner. The morning crowd was pressed together; coffee and breakfast odors, newspapers and conversation blended pleasantly. For the past several weeks Jason and his father had taken to coming out early for breakfast, prior to going their separate ways. The fragile truce seemed to be holding.

The past two meetings at Haven House and Overcomers had both focused upon making amends for offenses committed against others. Jason was stumbling through the process with his father, and was surprised at the results.

As they paused to eat a few bites, Jason thought about all he had accomplished. With Mike's help he had isolated lying, dishonesty, and covering-up as his major offenses against others and had managed to even apologize to his dad for these. They had been talking today about the cover-ups. It turned out that Jason hadn't been as slick as he thought. His father had known about most of it.

Dad cleared his throat. Jason had learned that this was a sign that his father was trying to say something difficult. "You know, your cover-ups didn't really upset me all that much."

Jason waited, then gave his father the required prompt, "Yeah?"

"Yeah. What was really hard was watching you and seeing myself in you."

That one stopped Jason. "What do you mean?"

"You did all the things I used to do to cover up." His dad chewed thoughtfully on some toast, looking away. "Things I still do. It was like watching all the dumb stuff I try to pull. I'd get mad because it was me." Tears of frustration welled up in his father's eyes, only to be quickly dismissed. "It was like God playing a joke on me. I wasn't so much mad at you. I sort of figured all kids do that. I was mostly mad at myself."

Jason looked down, absently playing with his eggs.

His dad continued. "But your mother . . . she was the one who was hurt. She'd come into our room and cry. Did you know that?"

Jason didn't.

"She's the one you need to talk to."

Jason was quiet again. "Dad, there's another thing I need to take care of and I need your help. Remember when I went AWOL from Haven House?"

His dad nodded, looking at him.

"Well this is hard for me to tell you, but I stole a car and got into an accident." His dad waited. "I need your help in figuring out what to do."

▼ ▼ ▼

Later that morning at school, Jason was walking between classes. As he came around a corner, he almost collided with someone coming the other way. He hadn't been paying attention, but as they stepped around one another, Jason realized who it was.

The other guy looked quickly down and slipped away. "Hey," called Jason, "aren't you—?"

"What's up?" asked one of Jason's friends.

"That guy," asked Jason, pointing. "What's his name?"

"Ronny Jacobs. Why?"

Jason tried to catch up, but lost Ronny in the crowd.

▼ ▼ ▼

The late afternoon sun warmed Mike's office. "How's the 'amends business' going?" asked Mike, leaning back and playing with a pencil.

"It's weird," Jason said. "I've been going out for breakfast with my Dad. That's working great! We've never talked like this before. But I just can't bring myself to apologize to my mother. And there's this guy at school . . ."

"Let's start with your mom," Mike interjected.

"I'd rather talk about the guy at school."

"I'm sure you would," smiled Mike. "What's up with your mom?"

"I don't know. I know that my drinking and messing up at school hurt her a lot. My dad told me that. And I am sorry I hurt her. It's just that every time I go to tell her, something sticks in my throat and I just can't do it. I have to walk out."

"Maybe you're still too mad at her," suggested Mike.

"What do you mean?"

"Well, we've talked a lot about the way she and your dad would shut you out when they were having problems, and then act like nothing was wrong. You mentioned that they would expect you to pretend that you were just one happy family, when really you weren't. Yet you seem to be better able to forgive your father his shortcomings. Why not your mom? Did she do something especially hurtful to you? Is there something there you just can't forgive yet?"

Jason thought for a bit. The light was fading now and the room was growing darker. "You know," he said slowly, "there was one thing. When my mom and dad were fighting and I did something bad, she would just dump all over me." He grew more intense as the memory got clearer as to what it all meant. "She would throw up her hands and yell 'There, see? You're just like your father.' To her that meant bad, a bum, irresponsible. God, I hated that!"

"Why was that so bad?"

"Because of the way she felt about him. It meant that she felt that I was nothing but a problem, too. That I couldn't do anything right. That if it wasn't for me, everything would be OK." He thought for a minute more. "That I was nothing but a drunk."

Mike reached over and turned on the desk lamp. "It sounds to me like you're still too mad to ask for her forgiveness. It would mean caving in and admitting she was right about all the things she implied when she was mad."

Jason was quiet. His mom's implications may have been wrong, but Mike's were right. He needed to make amends to his mother to clear away old resentments. Recovery required it. But he would have to start by forgiving her for her shortcomings if he was going to be able to make amends for his.

157

"Now how about the guy at school?" asked Mike.

Jason got up and stretched. He told Mike about almost running into him in school, then settled back into his chair. "I met this guy at a party six months ago. We were both drinking and messing around. I was pretty drunk. I didn't like what the guy was saying, and we got into it."

Mike asked "You fought?"

"Well, I more or less beat him up. I sucker-punched him, and he never landed a blow."

"How bad was he?"

Jason spoke more softly. "Mike, I really don't know how bad he was. Nobody called the cops, and the guy just left. But someone said later that he wouldn't come back to school for a long time. He had a home teacher and everything. I think I did that to him."

"But you're not really sure," clarified Mike.

"No. But when I saw him the other day, he took off as soon as he saw it was me. I just don't feel good about it. I used to think that the alcohol did it, but that's not true. I did it."

"So what are you going to do about it?"

▼ ▼ ▼

Jason rang the doorbell. It was in the middle of the week, and past dinnertime. "He ought to be home," Jason thought.

The porch light came on, and the door latch clicked. It finally opened, and Ronny Jacobs looked out through the chain lock. When he saw who it was, he tightened. "Listen—you'd better leave me alone or I'm calling the cops. You'd better leave." The door started to close.

"Wait a minute, Ronny, I just came here to talk! Please hear me out." A few moments passed. The door opened again, the chain lock still in place.

"What do you want?"

"Ronny, I need to talk to you about the fight."

KATHY

"Excuse me!" Kathy called out, hurrying to catch up with the three girls leaving class. Regina and her friends turned, bracing for trouble. Kathy and Regina had had words in class. After some time Kathy had cooled off, and she wanted to handle this one differently. Her workbook had outlined a way, and she wanted to try it out. While she didn't feel at the time that this incident was really all that big, or even all her fault, it certainly was no bridge to die on.

"Regina," she started. "I shouldn't have gotten mad back there. It wasn't a big deal. I'm sorry."

"You'd better be sorry, or it will be a big deal," glowered Regina.

"Sorry. There's only one thing around here that's sorry, and that's you!"

"Look," tried Kathy again, "I'm just trying to apologize. Let's be friends, OK?"

"Make friends? Where do you get off? First you drive everyone crazy, then you come in and figure everything's fine. You've made too many people mad. Girl, you got no friends here!"

That one hit home. Kathy was paralyzed; she didn't know what to do. She was angry enough to lash out. She felt humiliated and wanted to run. A crowd was forming.

Time slowed. She had fought before, and figured that she could probably do OK against Regina. There was a time when she wouldn't even hesitate. So what was different this time? She saw that Regina wouldn't, couldn't back down with the crowd around them. Nor could she. Or could she? "What do I really want, here?" she asked herself. "Perhaps . . . . "

"Regina, you're right. I *have* been a pain. I'm working on changing that, and maybe I'll get it right some day. I'm sorry." And with that she abruptly turned and walked away. The onlookers murmured derisively and a few booed, but Regina and her friends just stood there.

▼ ▼ ▼

"So what happened today?" asked Nicole. They were cleaning up after dinner. "I heard you were in a fight."

"I guess it depends upon what you mean by a fight." Kathy related what had happened in first period English and afterwards. She told about nearly fighting and then finding a better way. "One thing that still bothers me," concluded Kathy, "the one thing that I just can't let go of is that Regina told me that I had no friends." She looked at Nicole, her eyes reflecting her pain. "Having friends has always been real important to me. I guess it's because I'm codependent, but I need others to like me."

159

Kathy paused and looked out the dark window to the streetlight beyond. "The most frightening thing in the world for me is rejection. But even that's not what really bothers me about this thing. Nicole, she seemed so sure that I had no friends. Just how many people have I hurt so that they don't like me? This business is a lot bigger than I thought." Kathy wanted answers that Nicole could not provide. "What am I supposed to do? Make separate apologies to every one I've ever known?"

Nicole said nothing.

"There's another problem," Kathy continued, pacing the kitchen. "I've got this grandmother in Fresno. She won't talk to me on the phone any more, but I owe her some serious apologies. I think she really did like me, but I used her to get back at my father. I don't know what I can do to make up for it, but I at least want her to know."

▼ ▼ ▼

Kathy stood before the class. It was the last five minutes of first period English. "I asked Ms. White if she would let me talk to all of you this period." Some class members groaned, a few shifted. Most, like Regina, didn't move. "I'm codependent," Kathy went on. "I've always believed that having people like me was the most important thing, so I pushed too much. I've done some really stupid things to get attention, and that has caused problems. I've been obnoxious, started fights, and disrupted class. For this I have to apologize. I'm sorry. From now on, please let me know if I'm doing that again." As she sat down in her seat it was very quiet.

The silence followed her down the hall after class. She hadn't really expected anyone to say anything, but it would have helped. She had never felt more alone in her life, and it was all she could do to stay.

There was a tap on her shoulder. One of the quieter girls whose name Kathy did not even know was walking beside her. "Thanks, Kathy. That must have been hard."

▼ ▼ ▼

"Thanks for bringing me down, Nicole!" The bus station was busy. Loading instructions echoed from loudspeakers, engines roared as buses pulled out, and diesel exhaust hung heavily in the cold air. Kathy turned back before climbing the steps into the Fresno bound 6:30 express. "I'll be back on Sunday night. Don't forget to pick me up!"

"I won't forget. You take care! Are you sure you should miss classes today?"

"I probably shouldn't, but I really have to do this."

INSIGHTS

When others hurt us, they owe us. They need to make it right through apologies and restitution. Restitution is payback. If someone does ten dollars worth of damage, that person owes ten dollars plus an apology for the inconvenience their action caused. And if we hurt others, we owe them. In the back of our mind we keep an account book, where we record what we owe others and what others owe us. If others owe us, we feel resentment. If we owe others, we feel shame and guilt. In order to be free emotionally, we need to settle past accounts.

Making amends is one of the most powerful tools we have to turn our problem behavior around. Through the amends-making process we defuse the shame that constricts us, set the stage for building healthy relationships, and open ourselves to a future full of new possibilities.

If we set out to climb a mountain, we need to take the gear for the climb. But if we take unnecessary baggage, we may never make it to the top. Our lives are no different. If we are carrying old hurts, old resentments, and old grudges, we waste our energy and cloud our vision. If we are carrying excess shame, guilt, and ongoing bad feelings, we can't make the moves in the world we need to make.

Shame and guilt are like pain. Pain lets us know when our bodies are being damaged so that we may take steps to protect ourselves. Feelings of shame and guilt are not bad. They let us know when we are hurting others. Like pain, they are tools we have for living well.

But like pain, shame and guilt can be unhealthy. Shame and guilt are unhealthy if they are undeserved, or if nothing can be done to relieve them. If you hurt someone who has since died, if someone made you feel shame when you had no reason to, or if there is nothing that can be done to make up for the harm, then there is no healthy reason to continue to carry around the shame or guilt. If unhealthy pain and guilt are slowing your recovery, then they must be unburdened.

By acknowledging the harm they have done in the past, Sylvia, Jason, and Kathy free themselves for their future. Sylvia melts the frozen relationship with her family, Jason lets go of his fight

161

with his family, and Kathy sets off to square things with her grandmother. They have each unburdened themselves inside and begun healing their relationships with family and friends.

Sylvia's parents reacted to receiving her picture in a way other than she had anticipated. Through her discussion with Dr. Perez, Sylvia came to understand how her behavior had done more damage to her parents than she had realized. In talking it over later with Louise, Sylvia remembered another relationship that had gone bad, largely due to her own actions. Knowing that she needed to make amends, she decided to talk to her parents directly. The old boyfriend was another story. She felt that no matter what she said, he would misinterpret her actions as an attempt to rekindle the relationship. Consequently, she decided to make her amends by letter.

Jason had a similar experience when amends to his father led to the discovery that his mother had been even more seriously affected. He had difficulty making amends to her, however, and learned through Mike the extent of his anger at her. He was in no position to make amends until he had come to grips with that anger. In addition, he ran into someone his own age whom he had hurt through misdirected anger. The amends-making process is teaching Jason much about himself.

Kathy struggled with learning new ways to relate to people. Like Sylvia and Jason, she found that she had alienated many people around her. If she was to get her life back on track, she was going to have to work at making things right with them. Although her problems were extreme, she was willing to take extreme measures to solve them. Confronting her entire class and traveling a long distance to see a grandmother she had offended were efforts she was willing to make.

162

In the process of making amends, each of the three is discovering the extent of the harm done. Each is learning more about him- or herself. And each is working out his or her own way to rebalance the social scales. Making amends is necessary to them, and is necessary to you, to pave the way toward constructive and healthy relationships.

EXERCISES

If you are going to settle past accounts, if you are going to make amends for past wrongs, do it right! Take the time to figure out just what it was you did and how best to apologize and make restitution. You will probably be nervous, and you may even put off doing it to avoid embarrassment or humiliation. But just remember, you have much more to gain from this than does the person to whom you will apologize.

Start by identifying the major incidents and just who was affected. Give some thought to the actual harm that was done. Be open to hearing from others, don't rely on not just your own memories. Decide what sort of apology to make and the best way to make it. Determine if more harm might be done by carrying out the apology, and select an alternative approach, such as asking someone to "stand in" for that person and hear your apology, if necessary. Take the process seriously, and you will get serious results.

What Happened?

There are many ways we can hurt people. Here's a partial list of offenses against others:

intolerance	stealing
arguing constantly	abuse
immorality	irresponsibility
fighting	exploding
overcommitting	insulting or name-calling
displacing anger	being dishonest
withdrawing	making demands
controlling	being helpless
breaking promises	being jealous
making fun of	being self-centered

We all have done some of these things. Some of us have done all of them. Often nothing comes of it, but sometimes we do real harm. You probably don't need to make amends for every offense against another person, but there are incidents which have been particularly hurtful. These require action in order to clear your conscience and your relationships.

From the list above, search back in your memories for specific incidents. Think about how old you were at the time, who was involved, and what you did. Remember that it is easy to forget incidents and to underestimate the harm you have done. Take the time necessary to explore your own memories and talk to others about your actions in the past. Talk to relatives or friends who have known you for a long time. Tell them about your project and ask them if they can recall incidents in which you hurt others. Be particularly open to their comments and perspectives about the effects of your actions. It is easy to forget things about which we are not proud.

As you remember or learn about incidents, make notes on each. Make an estimate of the damage you think you did to that person. Consider the damage inflicted at that time, the damage that may have surfaced later, and the way in which the incident damaged your relationship over time.

There are three types of current pain caused by past actions:

▼ The victim of our hurtful actions may still be experiencing pain

▼ We may be experiencing shame

▼ Our relationship may be impaired

Space is provided on pages 165-166 for six separate incidents. You may not need them all. If you need more, make a copy of the form and keep it in your notebook or tape it to the inside back cover of this book.

*A*mends

164

Once you have a list of incidents requiring amends, your work is cut out for you. You have created an inventory of people with whom you need to clear things up. While this list may grow as you recall incidents or learn about pain you have caused, you have a starting point. It is time to decide how and when to make amends to those on your list.

Amends have two components. First, you must acknowledge what you have done and apologize for having done it. Second, you must attempt to make restitution for the *(continued on page 167)*

Incident #1: Approximate date of incident: _____

Who was involved: _____

_____

What I did: _____

What damage I did: _____

_____

_____

_____

· ·

Incident #2: Approximate date of incident: _____

Who was involved: _____

_____

What I did: _____

What damage I did: _____

_____

_____

_____

· ·

Incident #3: Approximate date of incident: _____

Who was involved: _____

_____

What I did: _____

What damage I did: _____

_____

_____

_____

Incident #4: Approximate date of incident: _____

Who was involved: _____

_____

What I did: _____

_____

What damage I did: _____

_____

_____

_____

. . . .

Incident #5: Approximate date of incident: _____

Who was involved: _____

_____

What I did: _____

_____

What damage I did: _____

_____

_____

_____

. . . .

Incident #6: Approximate date of incident: _____

Who was involved: _____

_____

What I did: _____

_____

What damage I did: _____

_____

_____

_____

damage you have done. Just how you do either of these, however, will vary according to the person, the incident, and the way things stand at present.

The apology consist of acknowledging what occurred and accepting responsibility for having done it. It lets the other person know he or she was not to blame for getting hurt. Apologies restore the personal dignity of the person who was hurt.

The restitution consists of attempting to pay back for the damages. Fixing or replacing damaged property, or paying money may be appropriate. If money or property were stolen, they should be returned. Sometimes the things damaged are irreplaceable. Sometimes time or effort can be acceptable as partial restitution. Because each situation differs, creativity may be required to make restitution.

Usually amends are made face-to-face. The basic message is "I did it, I'm sorry, I'd like to hear your side of it, and here's what I'm going to do to try and make up for it." An essential part of the amends-making is listening to the other person and learning what the incident meant to him or her. Much can be learned from this.

Pick a location and time when you are not likely to be disturbed or distracted.Try following these steps:

▼ Tell the person what you are about to do

▼ Describe the situation as best you remember it

▼ Describe your actions as you remember them

▼ Describe what you imagine he or she feels

▼ Tell how you feel now about having done it, admitting full responsibility for your actions

▼ Say the words: "I am sorry for _____"

▼ Inquire as to what he or she felt at the time, and later

▼ Invite him or her to discuss the incident with you later

Sometimes making amends can cause further harm. Normally amends-making includes a full disclosure of the incident. If full disclosure would hurt the recipient more, hurt a third party unnecessarily, cause family turmoil, damage reputations, or in any way be harmful, then it should not be done.

In such cases a partial disclosure may be possible. Partial disclosure would include only that information necessary for the apology, or only that part of the information that would not be hurtful. In cases where information must be left out, restitution would best be made by more loving, considerate and responsible behavior.

Space is provided on pages 169–171 for you to make plans for making amends for the six incidents you have already written about. Again, you may not need them all, or you may need to make copies of the forms and keep them in your notebook.

Indirect Amends   When making amends would be hurtful to the person or to someone else it is probably better not to try. But then you yourself are deprived of the healing process. In such cases some indirect methods of making amends can help. These can be done alone or with other, non-involved people present. Here are some alternatives to try:

By yourself:

▼ Sit in front of an empty chair. Close your eyes and imagine the person to whom you need to make amends sitting opposite you. Say what you would have said had he or she really been there. Imagine the person's response. Talk it out fully.

▼ Imagine yourself before a group. Give a speech to them, in which you disclose your actions and make amends.

▼ Talk to a picture of the person.

▼ Write a letter to the person. You can decide later whether or not to mail it.

▼ Write a dialogue with the person. Write your amends as if you were saying them, and write responses you think he or she might make.

▼ Write a dialogue that discloses the entire incident itself.

▼ Imagine, act, or write enlargements or extensions of the incident or of your making amends. Carry it into the future. *(continued on page 172)*

168

Incident #1

Plan for apology: _____

_____

Plan for restitution: _____

_____

Alternative, indirect apology if necessary: _____

_____

Date of amend-making: _____

How I felt at the time of making amends: _____

_____

His or her reaction: _____

What I learned: _____

_____

Other amends necessary: _____

· ·

Incident #2

Plan for apology: _____

_____

Plan for restitution: _____

_____

Alternative, indirect apology if necessary: _____

_____

Date of amend-making: _____

How I felt at the time of making amends: _____

_____

His or her reaction: _____

What I learned: _____

_____

Other amends necessary: _____

Incident #3

Plan for apology: _____

_____

Plan for restitution: _____

_____

Alternative, indirect apology if necessary: _____

_____

Date of amend-making: _____

How I felt at the time of making amends: _____

_____

His or her reaction: _____

What I learned: _____

_____

Other amends necessary: _____

. . . .

Incident #4

Plan for apology: _____

_____

Plan for restitution: _____

_____

Alternative, indirect apology if necessary: _____

_____

Date of amend-making: _____

How I felt at the time of making amends: _____

_____

His or her reaction: _____

What I learned: _____

_____

Other amends necessary: _____

Incident #5

Plan for apology: _____

_____

Plan for restitution: _____

_____

Alternative, indirect apology if necessary: _____

_____

Date of amend-making: _____

How I felt at the time of making amends: _____

_____

His or her reaction: _____

What I learned: _____

_____

Other amends necessary: _____

. . . .

Incident #6

Plan for apology: _____

_____

Plan for restitution: _____

_____

Alternative, indirect apology if necessary: _____

_____

Date of amend-making: _____

How I felt at the time of making amends: _____

_____

His or her reaction: _____

What I learned: _____

_____

Other amends necessary: _____

With others:

▼ Act out the incident, then stop your actions, apologize and make restitution on the spot.

▼ Role play your amends-making, using a stand-in to play the part of the person whom you injured.

▼ Look back at the exercise where you examined the hurt that each of your actions caused. For each incident, consider whether payback would help either you or the injured party, and what it would feel like to receive restitution. Finally, consider whether the restitution needs to be full, partial, or simply some token.

As you will discover in the next chapter, the amends-making process is never over. It is a fundamental building block of good relationships. Because you are human you will continue to make mistakes and hurt others. Learning to incorporate amends-making as an on-going part of living gives you the power to maintain a healthy support system for yourself.

9

Staying with the Program: Steps Ten through Twelve

You have worked through this book. You have spent days working on the questions and exercises, and weeks or even months shaking loose from the problem you came to solve. You came to grips with something bigger than you were, something that had your life in its control. And you have overcome it. So that's it, right?

Wrong. Very wrong. As much as we all would like the painful truth to go away, we need to hear it. And the painful news here is that old problems, like bad pennies, tend to come back. It is simply not enough to have broken bad habits. In order for your life to turn around, it must stay turned around. So, this chapter is about maintaining recovery. It is about preventing relapse into old patterns.

The urge to relapse—to fall back into your problem behavior—is and will be an ongoing, ever-present threat. You will go through periods of stress and trouble as a normal part of living, and you will be tempted to slide back into your problem behavior. This is a particular risk during adolescence because you are growing and changing so quickly. Pressures increase and life circumstances shift more quickly now than at any other time of life. This means that relapse is always a concern, and you need to have a relapse-prevention program. You need to adopt a strategy for dealing with the threat of relapse *now*. Fortunately, the steps you need to take are steps that will enhance your life in other ways.

Now in recovery and abstaining from their problem behaviors, Sylvia, Jason, and Kathy must confront their tendencies to return to their old ways. Through this process they find themselves not only strengthening their resolution, but enriching and empowering their lives.

Steps Ten, Eleven, and Twelve are relapse-prevention steps. While each focuses on a different strategy, together they form a powerful means by which you can avoid relapse. Step Ten incorporates honesty and responsibility. It reads:

10. Continue to make a personal inventory and when you are wrong admit it promptly.

Continuing the process of Steps Four and Five (making a personal inventory and admitting to yourself and others when you are wrong) and Steps Eight and Nine (making amends to those you have wronged) is central to maintaining recovery. By doing these things you stay clear within yourself and stay right with others.

Step Ten allows you to confront yourself and own up to your behavior. It also allows you to maintain positive working relationships with those around you. Your family and close friends can provide you with the support you need to stay in recovery.

JASON

"Hey! It's great to have you back, bro!" Aaron was lit and had his arm over Jason's shoulder. Jason had a beer in his hand. He couldn't believe what a relief it was to feel the alcohol setting in. He also couldn't believe how quickly it had happened.

Earlier that evening, Jason had been at home. He had been bored and jumpy. Unable to relax, he had picked a fight with his mother and stormed out. The party had been easy to find: he had just called Aaron.

Cindy Jameson brushed by him, and smiled invitingly. "Hi, Jason," she purred. "Got anything special tonight?" It was all so easy. He noticed the dreamy expression on her face and her vacant eyes. Jason smiled back and moved away.

The music was loud and the party spilled out into the backyard. Jason knew the police would inevitably be called. He gravitated toward the pool where things were a little less hectic. Small groups clustered here and there in the shadows and Jason looked for someone he knew. Breaking away from one group, a girl he used to know came over to greet him.

"Dominique!" called Jason. "How are you?"

"Never better!" She seemed genuinely happy to see him.

Jason held up his beer. "I was just going to get another. Want one?"

"No," she said. "I'm drinking a soda." She paused. "I had to quit."

"Quit?"

"Jason, I've been sober now for six months. I can't go back."

▼ ▼ ▼

"So what happened?" asked Mike.

Jason was not happy. "I was at a party. I had a beer."

"And . . . "

"Well, the good news is that I didn't get drunk."

" . . . and the bad news?" Mike was getting tired of "Twenty Questions."

"Mike, the bad news is that I would have. I met this girl there. She was in recovery, and we left and went out for coffee. We ended up talking until after midnight. I'm going to see her again."

"That's good."

"But if she hadn't been there I probably would have continued."

"What are you going to do next time?" Mike probed.

"She was drinking soda. That seemed OK. I could do that. And when it got uncomfortable, we just left. But I think that it wasn't so much *that* I was there but rather *why* I was there that matters."

"How so?"

Jason reddened. "I had gone because I got into a fight with my mother. It isn't important why, just that we did. I went to the party to get away from her."

"Maybe you got into the fight so you would have a reason to go to the party," suggested Mike.

▼ ▼ ▼

His mother was reading in the living room when Jason got home. Jason knew what he had to do but it still wasn't easy. He sat down opposite her and took a deep breath. "Mom," he said.

175

She looked up and regarded him with suspicion. The only time he started like this was when he wanted something or was setting her up for a fight. "Yes?"

"Mom, I need to tell you some things. Actually, I need to apologize."

"Apologize for what?"

"Last night . . . " he began.

▼ ▼ ▼

Jason found that his greatest trouble came when he drove a wedge between himself and his family and went off to party in order to avoid anxiety. This was an old pattern for which he had to be alert. When it happened, he had to take steps to correct it. This meant finding ways to handle both the situation and the damaged relationships that his behavior created.

While Step Ten involves continuing the processes of earlier steps and continuing to take inventory, Step Eleven aims at deepening spiritual life. It reads:

> 11. Use prayer and meditation to improve your conscious contact with your Higher Power, trying to understand that Power's will and asking for the power to carry that out.

Addictions or compulsions are often simply poor substitutes for spirituality. By deepening your spiritual life you provide for yourself what your addiction or compulsion provided for you; something bigger to rely upon. Church or religion may be one way to accomplish this. Alternatively, personal prayer, meditation, or other personal forms of spiritual expression may give you what you need. Inspirational or philosophical reading may be your way, or you might find someone to act as a mentor or teacher for you.

176

However you go about deepening your spiritual experience, whatever way works for you, *do* it. Find your own way, and you will fill the emptiness that your addiction or compulsion seeks to fill.

SYLVIA

Something was missing. Sylvia paced back and forth in her room. Everything had been going well. She was making new friends, things were going alright with her parents, but there was a familiar feeling of emptiness inside. Old cravings began again and she felt herself drawn to food.

She wandered down to the kitchen. No one was around, and there were some cookies in the cupboard. She stood by the sink for a while, feeling angry at herself for being unable to walk away, but the craving was strong. It would be so easy just to have one. Or maybe just a few. What started as a vague longing had turned into a major battle.

Sylvia picked up the phone and called Louise. After several rings Louise answered. They exchanged small talk for a while until Louise realized that something else was going on. "Why did you really call?" she asked.

"Oh, Louise, it's happening again. I'm standing here in the kitchen fighting with myself about whether or not to eat cookies. I'm so embarrassed."

"I'm glad you called, Sylvia. What do you think is going on?"

"I don't know. Nothing, really. Maybe that's the problem. Are you doing anything this afternoon?"

"Yeah," smiled Louise, "meeting with my best friend. Let's do something!"

"Thanks!" Sylvia was relieved.

"One more thing. Maybe it's time for another visit with Dr. Perez."

"But everything is going so well," protested Sylvia.

"Is it?"

▼ ▼ ▼

Sylvia sat in the waiting room at Dr. Perez's office. She fumed. "There's no reason for this," she thought. "Everything's been going so well. It's been three months since I was here. Now it's like I'm starting all over again. All this fuss over one little episode. And I haven't even eaten anything. So why have I come?"

Yet that moment at the sink had been real. She had felt the war raging within her. To eat or not to eat, that had been the question. Or at least it had appeared so at the time. Now it seemed more complicated. Why hadn't she been able to just walk away, or even to just eat in a sane and guilt-free way. Why the battle? And what was the emptiness and discontent all about in the first place?

Just then Dr. Perez opened the door to her office and smiled at Sylvia. "It's been a while! Come in—I've missed you." It was good to see Dr. Perez again and it felt reassuring to be ushered back into the room in which she had done so much work before.

"Now then," said Dr. Perez, settling in her seat. "Even though it's nice to visit, you're obviously here for a reason. What brings you back?"

Sylvia went directly to the point, recounting the incident at the sink and including the vague but unsettling feelings of emptiness and longing. "Really, Dr. Perez," she concluded, "I probably shouldn't be taking up your time with this."

"You know, Sylvia, you don't have to wait to be in a crisis to benefit from a visit. Sometimes more subtle signs show us we are ready for a breakthrough. Let's see what the cookie was all about," she suggested. "What was happening just before the craving started?"

"I was up in my room. I remember feeling bored and restless."

"Didn't you have anything to do?"

"Actually I did," recalled Sylvia. "I was supposed to be doing my homework. I had a test the next day and I guess I couldn't make myself do the work."

"Was the test in a class you dislike or are having trouble with?"

"No, I do OK in World History." She thought for a few minutes. There was something else. "It's just that I've been working hard for so long to make other people happy. There has to be more to life than eating, sleeping, and studying."

"Like having fun?" asked Dr. Perez.

"That too," smiled Sylvia. "But more than that. I want my life to go somewhere, to mean something. I need a direction."

"So you think your trouble the other night had something to do with a need for purpose?"

"I don't know. Maybe."

"And maybe the emptiness isn't about eating, and the craving isn't for food," suggested Dr. Perez.

178

"I think not," replied Sylvia slowly, "but knowing that doesn't make it go away. I want something so badly that I need to do something. I need to fill the emptiness."

Dr. Perez took her time finding just the right words. "Sylvia, perhaps it's time to start doing some serious searching. Take that need for purpose, direction, and fulfillment seriously. Go find what you need."

▼ ▼ ▼

The brochure had been sitting on a store counter downtown. It had caught Sylvia's eye as she was making some purchases for school, and as she read it she became more intrigued. "The Center for Spiritual Development," the brochure read, "is a nondenominational retreat for people seeking to increase their contact with the spiritual dimensions of their lives." One of the workshops advertised was specifically for young people, and was titled "Meditation and Recovery."

"This is it!" she said aloud. People brushed around her as she stood in the middle of the sidewalk reading the brochure. Sylvia found a phone booth, inserted the correct change, and dialed the number.

▼ ▼ ▼

Step Eleven concentrates on deepening your spirituality and maintaining your conscious contact with your Higher Power. Step Twelve provides a culminating, final step in the process of recovery: it challenges you to carry the message to others, to give away what was so freely given to you. It reads:

12. Try to use the insights you have gained through your spiritual awakening to carry this message to others who are in trouble.

Carrying the message to others, showing others the way toward healthy living, giving them the support they need to take the steps they need to take are noble acts. But you will be the one who truly gains the most. The best way to learn is to teach, and the best way to experience the life-changing power of recovery is to be a part of the recovery of another.

KATHY

"Nicole, you were wonderful to take me in when I needed help. I really hate to leave!" It was moving day for Kathy. She had been promoted to three-quarter time at the bookstore and had found a room with kitchen privileges to rent near school. Not wanting to wear out her welcome with Nicole's family, she had decided to take the room. She and Nicole would remain close.

"It was a pleasure!" Nicole hugged Kathy. "And it was good for me. Part of my own recovery consists of helping others. I used to think it was just a duty, but I've discovered that I get more out of it than anyone."

"I don't know if anyone could get more than I did. I owe you. I know I can never repay it."

"Just pass it along. Call me as soon as you get settled and I'll come over."

"See you!" Kathy had her suitcase and a box tied on the rack on the back of her bicycle. She made her wobbly way down the street.

▼ ▼ ▼

It was the third week in her new room. Her days were busy. School in the mornings and work at the bookstore until 6:00 P.M. and on weekends. She would see Nicole now and then, as well as a couple of new friends. Yet time seemed to drag. She had picked up a small, used TV of uncertain vintage at the local thrift shop and that provided her with some diversion.

But sometimes she would start to get desperate again. It would start quietly enough. A little boredom, some feelings of loneliness. Attempting to avoid the discomfort, she would ignore her feelings and look for entertainment. Then she would "forget" to call Nicole, get angry at people, and blame school or her job for not being just right.

At this point Kathy would start thinking about the bar down the street. Even though she didn't drink and wasn't old enough, she was tempted to go in to see what was happening. Perhaps she could meet someone interesting.

During these periods she would have trouble with friends at school. She would start backsliding into her old ways of stirring up trouble. Usually she caught herself in time to make the necessary apologies and she would get angry at herself for doing it. Work would become a problem, too, as she would get snippy with customers. The manager even talked to her once about it.

Her journal proved to be helpful. In it she could write about the events of the day, things which had happened long ago, and even her hopes and dreams for the future. Sometimes she would have different people talk to one another, or have herself saying things to them which she could never do in real life.

One evening she had written:

In my dream last night I was walking in the spring rain. I had come out of a dark forest into a beautiful meadow that stretched upwards to the foot of a high mountain. The mountain was covered with clouds, but I knew it was there, and I could hear streams rushing from glacier meltwater. Pink, yellow, and purple flowers pushed up from the long deep green grass, blooming in the light rain. The path I followed meandered upwards toward a waterfall and the peak beyond. As I paused for breath and looked up, the swirling clouds parted long enough to give me a glimpse of the stunning snow-covered mountain peak against a brilliant blue sky.

I feel as if I am on the right path. I think that I am going in the right direction. If only I can stay on the path and not lose my nerve or get lost following some false trail.

The dream haunted her. She knew it meant that her recovery was close at hand, even when she was feeling down. Her life was full of possibility even though there were perils. She also knew recovery was a day-to-day proposition.

Tonight, instead of giving in to the uneasy feelings, she chose to write in her journal again. It had become less of a report on what she had been experiencing and more of a process of problem-solving on paper. She found herself changing as she wrote. Kathy made the following entry:

I'm going crazy looking at this room. I keep thinking about going down to the bar, but I know that's a bad idea. I think the long evenings are the worst. Mr. Tabor at school was talking about the city voc. ed. courses. They have a medical assistant certificate course which starts next week. If I did that next year, I could make the same money in half the hours and still be able to start college. I think I'll do it.

I'm still wondering what Nicole meant when she said she got more out of helping me than I got. How could she, when I got so much?

▼ ▼ ▼

Kathy put on her coat and went for a walk. At the sidewalk, she turned in the opposite direction from the bar and proceeded uptown. As she walked she thought more about Nicole's befriending her. How could Nicole get something of value out of listening to her making mistakes and agonizing over situations which could obviously be changed? What could she, Kathy, get from listening to someone else?

Before she realized it, Kathy found herself near the community center where her CoDA meetings were held. She realized it had been some time since she had attended a meeting, and that one was now in progress. She considered going in, but hesitated. It seemed like such an effort and she had been doing so well. It wasn't that clear how going over the same material again could help her now, yet something inside told her that she should.

As she stood in front of the building wrestling with the decision, she became aware of someone sitting on a bench in the dark. Whoever it was sniffled quietly and Kathy realized that she was crying.

Kathy went over. "Excuse me. Are you OK?"

"Yes," the girl hesitated. "No—I don't know."

"Are you waiting for someone?"

"Not really."

Kathy wondered if the girl was planning to go into the meeting. "Listen," she said, sitting down, "my name's Kathy. Are you sure there isn't anything I can help with?"

The girl looked at her in the dark. "I don't know. I came here to go to a meeting. It's in there." She glanced at the center doors. "Now I'm not so sure. My name is Maria."

"Maria, did you hear about the meeting from someone?" Kathy thought that it might help her understand why Maria had come.

"A friend told me it might help. I'm kind of mixed-up right now."

Kathy thought of Nicole. "I'm going in," she offered. "If you need some moral support, we could go together."

▼ ▼ ▼

It is only in reaching out to another that Kathy will discover the strength to work her own recovery program. Ironically she, who has brought such trouble to others through her codependency, will be the one who will go on to provide the most help to others.

INSIGHTS

Jason, Sylvia, and Kathy discovered that their problem behaviors could return to haunt them. When things were not right, when they had encountered new life challenges, or when they were feeling the stress and anxiety of preparation for a new step in their personal development, they were suddenly vulnerable.

Most of us know that "once an alcoholic, always an alcoholic." This does not mean that an alcoholic will always drink. But it does mean that once a person has become addicted to alcohol, drying out does not guarantee that he or she will never become addicted again. The possibility of reverting is ever-present. Recovery from addictions and compulsions is never forever; it is always accomplished and maintained one day at a time.

And so it is with any problem behavior that becomes habitual. The temptation to revert to old ways of problem-solving is always there. If we do backslide—if we drink, go on eating binges, or whatever it is that we have spent so much time and effort in overcoming—it is called a relapse.

Steps Ten, Eleven, and Twelve are the most powerful way to prevent relapse. But they can't work alone. The common factor in most relapses is stress. We get ourselves into recovery because we want to be free from the chains of our problems. And once we have broken our problem cycles, staying free usually isn't an insurmountable problem. But when our lives become stressful, maintaining recovery becomes more difficult. It is when we are pounded by life and feel inadequate to go on that we are truly tempted to return to our old ways.

But how can you live a full, productive, and satisfying life without experiencing a certain amount of stress? You really can't. School is stressful, families are stressful, jobs are stressful, and relationships are stressful. It would be unrealistic and short-sighted to believe that you could, or even should, lead a stress-free life. Stress cannot be avoided, but it can be managed.

Handling stress must become a priority in your life. In order to handle it, you must first come to understand

▼ what stresses you out

▼ how you react to stress

▼ how to recognize early signs of a stress reaction

▼ what you can do to break the stress cycle

Design a system for beating stress. Think it through by yourself or with someone who can help. Use your stress-busting strategies and Steps Ten, Eleven, and Twelve to smooth out your life before relapse becomes a real threat.

Finally, have a plan in hand in case you do relapse, or find yourself threatened by relapse. Know who you will call and what steps you will take should you find yourself sliding back into behavior that you know is heading for trouble.

*E*XERCISES

When we are under stress, we tend to act out. That's when we do the very things we want to turn around. Handling stress constructively, then, is a cornerstone in making big changes for ourselves.

Sometimes we assume that stressful situations "out there" directly cause our stress reactions. If it were that simple, we could move to a deserted island, camp out, and all our problems would be solved. Unfortunately, not only is that not practical, but it ignores our own input into the stress cycle. Even Robinson Crusoe could have a nervous breakdown if he let himself! What we do in response to stressful situations can make them better or worse. And our own responses can be changed.

One person's challenge can be another person's stress—and vice versa! Whether or not past experiences or personal traits cause this difference is not important; rather, it's important that you have your own "stress profile" of things you handle better than most people and things you don't. You have your own "hot spots"—specific situations that trigger stress responses in you.

*I*dentifying Stress

Which situations do you encounter that you have trouble handling?

_____

_____

_____

_____

In assessing how you react to these stressors, and what could be done to manage them better, look for signs of:

▼ work overload

▼ overwhelming responsibilities

▼ inability to detach

▼ overinvolvement with peers

▼ performance problems

▼ withdrawal

▼ decreased satisfaction

Are You Overloaded with Work? Remember the children's story about the pot that wouldn't stop producing porridge until the old woman said "Stop, little pot, stop"? Sometimes it seems as if work expands the same way. Not only do students always seem to have more homework to do, many also have important activities outside of class. Sports take a great deal of commitment: that means time, money, and energy. Part-time work takes its share too. An adequate social life may not be "work," but it takes time and energy away from work, making work more demanding.

Further, many young people are perfectionists. They often lose sight of what to *reasonably* expect of themselves in a particular situation.

How about you? What kind of demands do you have upon your time and energy?

_____

_____

_____

To what extent are you being realistic in what you expect of yourself?

_____

_____

_____

If you are overloaded, which of your activities are first priority, and which are less essential?

Essential

_____

_____

_____

Important, but not essential

_____

_____

_____

Optional

_____

_____

_____

Often it helps to talk to someone who knows you, to gain perspective on what is and isn't most important. This person might also help you sort out what is reasonable to expect of yourself given your differing goals.

Who might such a person be? (Write down a couple of options.)

_____

_____

***D**o You Have Overwhelming Responsibilities?* Feelings of being overwhelmed by responsibilities are common to business executives, professionals, and young people. Because adolescence is a growing time, young people are continually being saddled with new responsibilities by parents, teachers, employers, and friends. These responsibilities or pressures are diverse and they often conflict with one another. List some of the pressures you feel, by source (where the pressure comes from, for example work, school, etc.) and the specific action or actions you feel you need to take:

Source	_Responsibility_
_____	_____
_____	_____
_____	_____
_____	_____
_____	_____
_____	_____

Go back and rate each of these pressures on a scale of 1–10, where 1 = no stress, 10 = extreme stress.

There are several things you can do about handling these pressures. First, look at the way you prioritized your work in the preceding section. Use the same classification for each of the responsibilities. Now, are each of the responsibilities you listed of equal importance? Which are less important and don't deserve as much energy?

Sometimes all it takes is a nudge to get started, and we can nudge ourselves by just writing down the first steps. This puts things in manageable perspective. Below, list the first steps you can take in fulfilling each of your four most important responsibilities. The first one is an example.

Responsibility: school work _____

Step #1   see teacher for assignment _____

Step #2   organize this week's homework _____

Step #3   do tonight's homework _____

Step #4   start reading _Moby Dick_ _____

Step #5   _____

Mark off each step as you do them. Celebrate your success, as each is important to the large task. Pay attention to what you have done, not just what remains to be done.

Find someone with whom you can share your progress, support, mutual assistance, and perspective.

Who might that person be?

Responsibility: _____

Step #1 _____

Step #2 _____

Step #3 _____

Step #4 _____

Step #5 _____

. . . .

Responsibility: _____

Step #1 _____

Step #2 _____

Step #3 _____

Step #4 _____

Step #5 _____

. . . .

Responsibility: _____

Step #1 _____

Step #2 _____

Step #3 _____

Step #4 _____

Step #5 _____

. . . .

Responsibility: _____

Step #1 _____

Step #2 _____

Step #3 _____

Step #4 _____

Step #5 _____

Do You Have Trouble Detaching? You are finding a particular situation, or several situations, stressful. So why can't you let go of the situation? What keeps you there, or keeps you so attached that you let it stress you out? What's the hook?

Sometimes we have special vulnerabilities to certain issues. For example, Jason had trouble getting along with authority figures because his parents were so inconsistent. His drinking was a way to challenge authority figures at school. This created constant difficulty at school, which in turn became increasingly stressful.

Sometimes we have something to prove. Kathy had to constantly prove to herself that she was acceptable. School was Kathy's proving ground, and she worked harder than anyone to be popular and have friends. Consequently no one took her seriously, and they often joked about how desperate she was.

Jason and Kathy were "hooked" by school situations that they found quite stressful.

Think for a moment: what is there about the situation(s) which you find stressful, that "hooks" you?

_____

_____

_____

If a banker invests everything in one investment, she is vulnerable to bankruptcy if things go sour. Similarly, your overinvestment in a stressful situation can leave you open to major stress.

What other things do you have going on in your life that are equally important to you but less stressful?

Perhaps you could take a little time off and spend it with these other, less stressful things. Schedule time for them. See friends or relatives who are not connected with the stressful situation. Make time to meet your other obligations. Find a way to get some rest and relaxation.

189

List three things you could do to detach:

_____

_____

_____

Are You "Too Involved" with Your Friends? In our early teens, when we are trying to figure out who we are apart from our families, we first start by identifying with groups of people our own age. This is a natural path along the road to independence. Often, however, that path becomes a trap for us. We become trapped by our friends if we become so involved with them that we lose ourselves, or sabotage our own goals, or fail to create our own unique identity. And without our own sense of who we are, we lack the personal resources to deal with difficult situations.

Are you able to see yourself apart from your group? List ten characteristics that separate you from them:

1. _____   6. _____
2. _____   7. _____
3. _____   8. _____
4. _____   9. _____
5. _____   10. _____

Does your group support those differences, or do you take heat because of them?

_____

How much of your free time do you spend with your friends and how much with yourself?

_____

Of the time you spend with yourself, how much is spent on activities and projects that are different from those of your friends?

_____

Would your group of friends support your taking up an activity that does not interest them?

_____

If you decide to put more energy into your study, work, or personal interests, how could you go about letting your friends know that you need to do that but that you still value them and plan to keep up your friendship?

_____

_____

_____

_____

*A*re *You Having Performance Problems?*　The problem with stress is that it trashes performance. The problem with poor performance is that it creates stress. Too much stress lowers concentration, short-circuits motivation, and drains away energy —each of which is essential to study, work, or athletic performance. Similarly, getting low grades, being fired, or being dropped from a team creates even more stress.

Sometimes sorting it through is like the chicken riddle: Which came first, the chicken or the egg?

Don't get discouraged; concentrate on coming up with a solution. You have nothing to lose if you try. List the chain of events leading up to the present situation. Referring back to Chapter Three might be helpful, but in any case, list the events, stressful conditions, and performance problems (school, work, or sports) in their order of occurrence:

_____

_____

_____

_____

Now for another chicken and egg routine:

What would happen to your stress level if you picked up your performance?

_____

What would happen to your performance level if you calmed down the stress level?

_____

What would keep you from working on both at the same time?

_____

_____

Are *You Withdrawing From Others?* There's an old saying that goes "If you want to avoid stress, don't get involved with your own life!" That's true, and we know it. So well, in fact, that we do it all the time. When we begin to burn out, we tend to do an interesting one-two move. First, we get more tenacious and dig in harder. We get tunnel vision and grimly plod forward in the situation, instead of sitting back and figuring out what's wrong. The second thing we do is become numb. We withdraw emotionally from the situation and ice over. In so doing, we tend to withdraw from others who might help us think it through and gain perspective. We may even dehumanize others in the situation (like teachers, employers, customers, even friends), and treat them like obstacles or objects.

Think back about a stressful situation you have experienced. Describe it very briefly:

_____

_____

Did you find yourself shutting down emotionally?

_____

_____

How might you have handled that situation differently?

_____

_____

Could you have approached anyone in that situation and asked him or her to help you think through what was going wrong?

_____

What kept you from doing it?

_____

Do You Experience Role Strain? Adolescence isn't all that easy! Some people still treat you like a kid. Some people treat you like an adult, holding you responsible for everything. Some people treat you like both.

Adolescents wear many hats. They are expected to be students at school, workers at work, jocks on the field, children at home, "men" and "women" in public. Up until a few years ago they were expected to fight and die for their country at eighteen, yet were not allowed to drink or vote like other citizens. The expectations others have of young people are often unclear and even contradictory. Role strain is the stress caused by having contradictory demands placed upon you by others, or by yourself.

Sylvia experienced serious role strain when her parents expected her to be both herself (the quiet, nonachieving little sister) and her deceased sister, Angela (the outgoing, superachieving older sister). She wasn't able to say no to either of these extremes.

Sometimes it's useful to sort through some of the role demands. List those you experience:

_____

_____

_____

Which of these are a little (or a lot) unclear?

_____

Which are contradictory?

_____

_____

193

There are several things you can do to relieve some of the pressure you feel caused by role strain.

First, you might try sitting down and clarifying your responsibilities with those people to whom you feel you owe something. Find out just what they expect. Look for opportunities to negotiate a more reasonable set of expectations.

You might start by getting clear with yourself what expectations you could more comfortably live with. Write down a compromise expectation, or an alternative way of handling the responsibility. For example, if Sylvia really wanted to achieve more she might set a target level of achievement more appropriate to herself than her sister. Or alternatively, she might seek to become accomplished in an area of her own interest.

Responsibility   *Alternative*

———————————————————   ———————————————————

———————————————————   ———————————————————

———————————————————   ———————————————————

Also, consider talking to someone else about your role responsibilities. He or she might have some suggestions about other ways of looking at your situation. Similarly, find someone to talk to about the pressures you feel, someone who could simply provide you support.

*A*re *You Experiencing Decreased Satisfaction?*   The bottom-line result of these stress reactions is unhappiness. We do the things we do in this world to be happy. When we experience work overload, overwhelming responsibilities, inability to detach, overinvolvement, performance problems, withdrawal, and role strain, we are not getting satisfaction out of our lives.

Can you honestly say that you have been very happy lately?

———————————————————————————————————

How long has it been since you felt deep satisfaction from school, work, or other activities?

———————————————————————————————————

As we have seen so far, the signs of stress affect our lives deeply, gradually turning them into unsatisfactory grinds. As one student put it: "Hey, it just wasn't fun anymore." We have also talked about a number of ways of rethinking our situations and taking action to make things better. More strategies will be presented later.

But first, try this simple experiment. List ten things you have done before that were satisfying and fun, or things which have looked like they might be fun to try:

1. _____   6. _____
2. _____   7. _____
3. _____   8. _____
4. _____   9. _____
5. _____   10. _____

Now select just one, and try it this week.

*B*eating the Stress Cycle

The stress cycle begins the moment we enter a potentially stressful situation. What we expect and how we interpret the situation directly affect our emotional reaction. This determines how we respond, which in turn makes the situation better or worse.

What Are Your Expectations?   Here are three ways your expectations can directly influence the stress level of any situation. First, your expectations of the situation itself shape the way you respond to it. When you expect a negative result, you act differently than when you expect a positive result. You often convey a negative attitude, act in a negative or defensive way, and give up trying to work constructively. This has a predictable effect; it is called "self-fulfilling prophecy." Because you expect it, you help create it.

Consider the most stressful situations you have to deal with. Choose one. What are some of the cues you pick up on first that tell you it is likely to become a problem?

195

_____

_____

At that point, what do you predict will be the outcome? What chance do you feel that the situation will not prove stressful?

_____

_____

Take the same situation again. This time, write a possible positive outcome for the situation so you do not suffer the negative consequences as before:

_____

_____

If you were to let yourself believe that this were not only possible, but likely, you would convey a more positive attitude, act in positive ways, and work constructively to bring about that result. Because you expected it, you would help create it. Experiment with this the next time the situation arises.

The second way your expectations can influence the situation is the performance you expect from yourself. My guess is that you are pretty hard on yourself. You probably don't really have a limit to what you feel you should do. If you think you could score a 10, and do so, you probably sit around afterwards nagging yourself for not getting an 11.

The third way expectations complicate the situation is the way in which you expect yourself to cope. When you mentally review a difficult situation, you often persecute yourself twice. First on the basis of your performance, and then again about whether or not you let it bother you. If you felt stress, you blame yourself and make the situation still worse.

Become aware of what goes on in your mind during times of stress. What you expect of the situation, your performance, and your reactions all heavily influence the stress you experience. You may find that a little self correction can magically turn mountains into molehills.

Do Your Feelings Get Out of Hand?   Once we get caught up in a situation that we expect will be difficult or we interpret as negative, we will react emotionally. Part of learning to break the stress cycle involves learning to handle our emotions. Some people feel that feelings are uncontrollable, but that is simply not the case. We have far more control over what we feel than most of us care to admit.

Feelings like anger or fear are a little bit like pain. They alert us to the fact that something is wrong. Yet unlike pain, we tend to worship anger or fear. We think of them as an overfilled reservoir that must be drained to avoid damage. Thus we believe that we must

- ▼ "talk it out"
- ▼ "vent our frustration"
- ▼ "blow off steam"
- ▼ "cry"
- ▼ "explode"

Yet, research on emotions does not support this. Studies suggest that venting anger tends to produce more anger. "Talking it out" tends to keep people emotionally aroused. Further, high blood pressure, which we used to feel was connected to "keeping feelings in," is really connected to age, race, social class, and to the cause of the anger.

This does not mean that you shouldn't express your feelings. Getting in touch with how you really feel is an important part in deciding how to handle any situation. It just means that expressing the feelings doesn't solve anything. It also means that when you get frustrated, angry, hurt, or sad, you should not just sit around raging or weeping. Getting stuck in the feelings is a sure way to lose control of the situation.

The only thing that really provides a healthy expression of feelings is using that energy to *change* whatever was causing the feelings in the first place. Treating anger, or fear, or sadness as if the feeling is the problem is to misunderstand a natural process. It is like taking an aspirin to reduce the pain when your shoe is too tight.

Sometimes we find ourselves unable to take positive action because our feelings have gotten out of hand. At that point we need some strategies to manage our feelings until we can get back into control. Here are twelve ways:

1. Admit to yourself how you feel.

2. Decide where and when you could better express those feelings, and promise yourself that you will. Follow through.

3. If you have time, take a break and get away from the situation for a while.

4. Talk to someone not connected with the situation; gain perspective.

5. Do some deep breathing or relaxation exercises.

6. Use positive self-messages.

7. Write out what you see happening. Try to work out a plan on paper.

8. Try to figure out what you are really afraid of in the situation and how you can better take care of yourself.

9. Try acting as if you were feeling differently. "Fake it till you make it."

10. Listen to the messages your body sends.

11. Create an image of good outcome for the situation. Focus on that image.

12. Think about what kind of help you need and how to get it.

Which of these strategies sound good to you? Write them, or some of your own, below:

_____

_____

_____

Do You Take Effective Action? The bottom line in stress-busting is whether or not we make the situation worse. Coping strategies may have short-range success but may also create long-range problems. An example is alcohol. When we drink, we change our mood and relax. Things seem better. This makes the tension and uncertainty less bothersome. But down the road we pay. We may suffer a hangover, become addicted, or blow it socially. More importantly, we never learn to handle the situation in the first place.

Think about the major problem situations in your life. What sort of things did you do to cope with them?

Situation   *Response*

_____   _____

_____   _____

_____   _____

_____   _____

_____   _____

_____   _____

Looking back on those problem situations, how effective was your response? That is, did your action make the situation better in the long run, or worse? Did it have a positive effect on your life or not?

Rate the effects on a 1–10 scale, where 1 = the worst possible situation and 10 = the best outcome possible:

Situation 1 _____

Situation 2 _____

Situation 3 _____

Situation 4 _____

Here is an approach to positive action. Use the following steps to plan your attack. Do some analysis, decide what help you need, plan your approach, and then review the outcome of your actions.

Ask yourself the following questions:

▼ What is going wrong in this situation?

▼ What is the worst possible outcome for me?

▼ What is the more likely outcome?

▼ What am I doing to make the problem worse?

▼ What would I like to have happen?

▼ What specific steps could I take to make that happen?

Get some help:

- ▼ Find out who might be helpful
- ▼ Find out who has dealt successfully with this problem before
- ▼ Talk to them

Plan your attack:

- ▼ Consider some alternatives
- ▼ Decide what you want to do
- ▼ Break it down into steps
- ▼ Rehearse
- ▼ Take first things first
- ▼ Focus on one thing at a time

Check the results:

- ▼ Make spot checks halfway through
- ▼ Treat it like an experiment
- ▼ Rethink and regroup

Now look back at your situations from page 195 again. Think about how you might handle them differently. What could you have done then, or what could you do in the future to make them turn around?

Situation 1

_____

_____

_____

Situation 2

_____

_____

_____

Situation 3

_____

_____

_____

Situation 4

_____

_____

_____

Finally, in case you still haven't found just the right strategies which would work for you, here are thirty-three more! Circle any that you think might be useful.

be yourself	share more
get more variety in your life	meet some new people
visualize attractive futures	don't put things off
set yourself up for enjoyment	change your pace
do some good things for others	take naps
cut the criticism	let go
exercise your spirituality	focus on your goals
turn it over to a Higher Power	start a journal
meditate	pursue a new interest
give yourself good rewards	exercise
take care of your health	set limits for yourself
sleep enough	play
make necessary changes	consider alternatives
gain an attitude of gratitude	see a counselor
pay attention to your dreams	find a sanctuary
don't do things that hurt you	face fears
surround yourself with good friends	

*D*esign *a Relapse Prevention Plan*

When we perceive and interpret a situation as threatening, our nervous system starts a complex arousal process. This arousal leads to emergency behavior and further emotional upset. Sometimes this is lifesaving, but usually it gets us into trouble. Relapse into habitual problems is frequently the result of temporary stress. The key to dealing with such overwhelming reactions is early awareness. This buys us time to change thought patterns, to take action, to change the situation, to work at handling the feelings, or to change the response itself. Having a plan is essential. If you can gain control over the stress response, you will gain the upper hand in the battle to keep yourself turned around.

Look back over your answers to the questions in the last section. Use them to design your own plan to prevent relapse:

What situations have proven themselves particularly stressful to you in the past or what situations do you anticipate to be stressful in the future?

_____

_____

_____

_____

What steps have you learned to take to manage those situations? (*Hint:* look at your answers to the previous section, page 199.)

_____

_____

_____

_____

What personal reactions have you found to indicate that you are too stressed? (Look at your answers to the questions in the beginning of the exercise section of this chapter.)

Are there other signs to look for that indicate that you are at risk for relapse? Consider the answers to the question above, plus the following:

minimizing risk of relapse
being ungrateful
covering up
visiting old haunts
being depressed or full of anxiety
lying
being drawn to temptation
lacking faith
having performance problems
rejecting advice given by people in recovery
being preoccupied with thoughts of the problem behavior
spending more time with friends who share the problem

List the signs you know will be indications that you are at risk:

_____

_____

_____

_____

What steps can you take when you recognize that you are becoming at risk? How about if you actually do relapse?

_____

_____

_____

_____

In designing an action plan for relapse, first stop and remember what you initially did to break your habit. It obviously
worked, so start there. If you attended meetings, begin again. If
you saw a therapist, reschedule a visit. If certain people were
particularly supportive and helpful to you, look them up. If you
followed a program from a book, dust it off again. Whatever
worked the first time met a need that may be going unmet
again.

In addition, look at your past work in this book. Review
sections you found useful. Rework some of the exercises. Look
over plans you made and see if you really carried them out. Is
something being neglected?

Bear in mind that you may be changing again. Just as Sylvia's urge to relapse was really a sign that she was ready to move ahead in her personal development, your relapse urges may be a signal of your own readiness for new challenges. You may be ready to come to grips with forgotten parts of your past, new aspects of the present, or even the future. Getting clear on the origin of your distress helps you determine what to do to relieve it.

As you make plans for dealing with urges to relapse, review all the activities and suggestions you have considered in prior chapters to answer the question "What shall I do now?"

List the activities you will try and the people you will contact when the urge to relapse becomes strong:

Activities   *People (Phone number)*

_____   _____

_____   _____

_____   _____

_____   _____

_____   _____

_____   _____

What sort of amends can you make when your behavior has caused hurt to others? If you have relapsed, or even if the urge to relapse has been difficult, you may have offended or harmed others. Review the exercises on making amends from Chapter Eight; list the ways you will make amends to those you harm:

_____

_____

_____

_____

_____

Relapse is not the end of the line. It does not mean that you or your program are a failure. Relapse is a temporary setback. If you have relapsed, obviously something is wrong and needs attention. Get back into your program, work your steps, explore old business and new stressors.

It was mentioned at the beginning of this book that the Twelve-Step recovery program is the most powerful recovery program there is. That is true. But it is more. The Twelve-Step program, and indeed recovery itself, is more than just abstinence. Recovery is not about control over the parts of your life that are out of control. Recovery is the beginning of your new life. Through self-awareness, personal empowerment, satisfying relationships, and personal contact with your Higher Power, the real you is set free. Once you turn yourself around—anything is possible!

Resources

The main resources for dealing with overwhelming behavior problems are Twelve-Step programs in your area. Most are free, effective, and available. Some, such as Alcoholics Anonymous, Alateen, Narcanon, and Overeaters Anonymous, are problem-specific—you can usually tell by the name what the group focuses on. Others such as Overcomers Anonymous are open to anyone, irrespective of the nature of their compulsive problem. Most have meetings for young people. The best way to find them is to look in the white pages of the telephone book. Try looking under the heading that fits your problem, although the people at A.A. Central Office usually know about the others and can direct you to them.

Confide in those family members you have found trustworthy in the past. Look to school counselors, ministers and pastors, and youth workers as possible resources for you. Ask people you know who are in recovery for people they have found to be helpful.

In addition, look for a recovery section in your local bookstore, or look for a bookstore specializing in recovery literature. Continue your reading and work on recovery issues in your life.

The following hotlines provide information, referrals, and sometimes crisis intervention by telephone. The numbers are all toll free and the name of the organization reflects its specialty.

207

AIDS ALL Prevention Center   1-800-322-8911

AIDS Hotline   1-800-551-2728

Alcohol 24-Hour Helpline   1-800-252-6465

BASH Bulimia Anorexia Self-Help   1-800-227-4785

Child Help National Child Abuse Hotline   1-800-422-4453

Cocaine Hotline   1-800-262-2462

Covenant House   1-800-999-9999

Eating Disorder Hotline   1-800-233-5450

Food Addiction Hotline   1-800-872-0088

National Childabuse   1-800-4-A-CHILD (1-800-422-4453)

National Council of Compulsive Gambling   1-800-552-4700

National Institute on Drug Abuse   1-800-662-4357

National Runaway Hotline   1-800-231-6946

Runaway Hotline   1-800-448-4663

STD Hotline   1-800-227-8922

The following Twelve-Step anonymous groups have meetings in various communities nationwide. To find a meeting in your area look in the white pages of the telephone directory or call a local hospital or police department.

Adult Children Anonymous

Adult Children of Alcoholics

Alcoholics Anonymous

Alanon (families of alcoholics)

Alateen (teenagers)

Alatot

Bulimics/Anorexics Anonymous

Child Abusers Anonymous

Cocaine Anonymous

Codependents of Sex Addicts

Families Anonymous (families of drug users)

Narcotics Anonymous

Overeaters Anonymous

Overcomers Anonymous

Parents Anonymous (abusing parents, abused children)

Pills Anonymous

Sex Addicts Anonymous

Sexaholics Anonymous

Sex and Love Addicts Anonymous

Shoplifters Anonymous

Smokers Anonymous

Spenders Anonymous

The following organizations can also provide information on the areas of their interest. Write or call and ask them for what you need.

Adult Children of Alcoholics
Central Service Board
P.O. Box 35623
Los Angeles, CA 90035   Tel. (213) 464-4423

Al-Anon Family Group Headquarters
1372 Broadway
New York, NY 10018-0862   Tel. (212) 302-7240

Alateen
1372 Broadway
New York, NY 10018-0862   Tel. (212) 302-7240

Alcoholics Anonymous (A.A.)
General Service Office
PO Box 459
Grand Central Station
New York, NY 10163   Tel. (212) 686-1100

American Council on Alcoholism
8501 LaSalle Road, Suite 301
Towson, MD 21204   Tel. (301) 296-5555

American Council for Drug Education
204 Monroe Street
Rockville, MD 20850   Tel. (301) 294-0600

ALMACA: Association of Labor Management Administrators and
        Consultants on Alcoholism, Inc.
1800 N. Kent Street, Suite 907
Arlington, VA 22209   Tel. (703) 522-6272

AMSAODD: American Medical Society on Alcoholism and Other
        Drug Dependencies
12 West 21st Street, 7th Floor
New York, NY 10010   Tel. (212) 206-6770

Chemical People Project/WQED-TV
4802 Fifth Avenue
Pittsburgh, PA 15213   Tel. (412) 622-1491

Children Are People, Inc.
Chemical Abuse Prevention Program
493 Selby Avenue
St. Paul, MN 55102   Tel. (612) 227-4031

COAF: Children of Alcoholics Foundation, Inc.
200 Park Avenue, 31st Floor
New York, NY 10166   Tel. (212) 351-2680

Emotions Anonymous
P.O. Box 4245
St. Paul, MN 55104   Tel. (612) 647-9712

Families Anonymous
World Service Office
PO Box 528
Van Nuys, CA 91408   Tel. (818) 989-7841

Families in Action Drug Information Center
3845 N. Druid Hills Road, Suite 300
Decatur, GA 30033   Tel. (404) 325-5799

Gamblers Anonymous
P.O. Box 17173
Los Angeles, CA 90017   Tel. (213) 386-8789

The Grief Recovery Institute
8306 Wilshire Boulevard, Suite 21-A
Beverly Hills, CA 90211   Tel. 1-800-445-4808

Hazelden Foundation
Box 11
Center City, MN 55012   Tel. 1-800-328-9000

ICAA: American International Council on Alcohol and Addiction
PO Box 489
Locust Valley, NY 11560   Tel. (516) 676-1802

Incest Survivors
P.O. Box 5613
Long Beach, CA 90800

Johnson Institute
7151 Metro Boulevard
Minneapolis, MN 55435   Tel. (612) 944-0511

MADD: Mothers Against Drunk Driving
National Headquarters
669 Airport Freeway, Suite 310
Hurst, TX 76053-3944   Tel. (817) 268-6233

MIBCA: Minnesota Institute on Black Chemical Abuse
2616 Nicollet Avenue South
Minneapolis, MN 55408   Tel. (612) 871-7878

Multi-Cultural Prevention Work Group
Allegheny County MHMR/DA Program
429 Forbes Avenue, 9th Floor
Pittsburgh, PA 15219   Tel. (412) 355-4291

NAATP: National Association of Addiction Treatment Programs,
        Inc.
2082 Michelson Drive, Suite 304
Irvine, CA 92715   Tel. (714) 476-8204

NACOA: National Association for Children of Alcoholics, Inc.
31706 Coast Highway, Suite 201
South Laguna, CA 92677-3044   Tel. (714) 499-3889

NADAC: National Association of Alcoholism and Drug Abuse
        Counselors, Inc.
3717 Columbia Pike, Suite 300
Arlington, VA 22204   Tel. (703) 920-4644

NALGAP: National Association of Lesbian and Gay Alcoholism
        Professionals, Inc.
204 West 20th Street
New York, NY 10011   Tel. (212) 807-0634

Narcotics Anonymous
World Services Office, Inc.
PO Box 9999
Van Nuys, CA 91409   Tel. (818) 780-3951

NASADAD: National Association of State Alcohol and Drug Abuse
        Directors, Inc.
44 North Capitol. Street, N.W., Suite 520
Washington DC 20001   Tel. (202) 783-6868

NBAC: National Black Alcoholism Council
417 South Dearborn, Suite 700
Chicago, IL 60605   Tel. (312) 341-9466

NCA: National Council on Alcoholism, Inc.
12 West 21 st Street, 7th Floor
New York, NY 10010   Tel. (212) 206-6770

NCADI: National Clearinghouse for Alcohol and Drug Information
1776 East Jefferson Street
Rockville, MD 20852   Tel. (301) 468-2600

NCCA: National Clergy Council on Alcoholism
1200 Varnum Street, N.E.
Washington, DC 20017   Tel. (202) 832-3811

National Association for Children of Alcoholics
31582 Coast Highway, Suite B
South Laguna, CA 92677   Tel. (714) 499-3889

National Coalition for the Prevention of Drug and Alcohol Abuse
Quest International
6655 Sharon Woods Boulevard
Columbus, OH 43229   Tel. (614) 882-6400

National Coalition of Hispanic Health and Human Services
      Organizations
1030-15th Street, N.W., Suite 1053
Washington, DC 20005   Tel. (202) 371-2100

National Congress of Parents and Teachers (PTA)
700 North Rush Street
Chicago, IL 60611-2571   Tel. (312) 787-0977

National Federation of Parents for Drug-Free Youth
8730 Georgia Avenue, Suite 200
Silver Spring, MD 20910   Tel. 1-800-554-KIDS

NIAAA: National Institute on Alcohol Abuse and Alcoholism
Parklawn Building, Room 16-105
5600 Fishers Lane
Rockville, MD 20857   Tel. (301) 443-388

NIDA: National Institute on Drug Abuse
Parklawn Building, Room 10-05
5600 Fishers Lane
Rockville, MD 20857   Tel. (301) 443-4577

PRIDE: National Parents Resource Institute on Drug Education
Robert W. Woodruff Volunteer Service Center
100 Edgewood Avenue, Suite 1002
Atlanta, GA 30303   Tel. (404) 658-2548

Nation Prevention Network
c/o NASADAD
444 North Capitol Street, N.W., Suite 520
Washington, DC 20001   Tel. (202) 783-6868

NNSA: National Nurses Society on Addiction
2506 Gross Point Road
Evanston, IL 60201   Tel. (312) 475-7300

Overeaters Anonymous
World Service Office
2190 90th Street
Torrance, CA 90504   Tel. (213) 542-8263

RID: Remove Intoxicated Drivers
PO Box 520
Schenectady, NY 12301   Tel. (518) 372-0034

Rutgers University Center of Alcohol Studies Library
PO Box 969
Piscataway, N.J. 08854   Tel. (201) 932-4442

SADD: Students Against Drunk Driving
P.O. Box 800
277 Main Street
Marlboro, MA 01752   Tel. (617) 481-3568

Women for Sobriety, Inc.
PO Box 618
Quackertown, PA 18951   Tel. (215) 536-8026

Suggested Reading

Brondino, Jeanne, et al. (1988). *Raising Each Other: A Book for Teens and Parents.* Claremont, CA: Hunter House Inc.

Buckingham, Robert William and Sandra Huggard (1991). *Coping with Grief.* New York: Rosen.

Fleming, Martin (1991). *How to Stay Clean and Sober: A Relapse Prevention Guide for Teenagers.* Minneapolis, MN: Johnson Institute.

Gordon, Sol (1988). *When Living Hurts.* New York: Dell.

Hipp, Earl (1985). *Fighting Invisible Tigers: A Stress Management Guide for Teens.* Minneapolis, MN: Free Spirit Publishing.

Vedfal, Joyce, Ph.D. (1986). *My Parents Are Driving Me Crazy.* New York: Ballantine Books.

Wessen, Carolyn McLenahen (1988). *Teen Troubles: How to Keep Them from Becoming Tragedies.* New York: Walker and Co.

Zareck, David and James Sipe (1986). *Can I Handle Alcohol/Drugs? A Self-Assessment Guide for Youths* Minneapolis, MN: Johnson Institute.

Printed in the USA
CPSIA information can be obtained
at www.ICGtesting.com
JSHW082203140824
68134JS00014B/394